GREAT MISCHIEF

JOSEPHINE PINCKNEY

Great
Mischief

NEW YORK · THE VIKING PRESS

1948

813.4
P647g

PRINTED IN U.S.A.
BY H. WOLFF, NEW YORK

Part One

TOWARD the end of the last century, a time already remote enough to make fables seem possible yet near enough our day to share its commonplaces, a druggist by the name of Timothy Partridge kept a modest shop, too modestly tucked away in a narrow side street. The thirty-sixth year of his life doubtless appeared to him as humdrum and unremarkable as this of ours, except that Partridge, in a more credulous age, was a believer in the remarkable. Being a trained pharmacist, he believed in the marvels of science and in what he could see, smell, and weigh on his brass scales; but he also believed in realities not measured in drams and scruples, including the strict doctrines of his Church and other matters less pleasing to orthodoxy.

An evening in winter with a sodden rain falling seemed a time for dealing with what is generally considered factual. A thin gas pipe descended from the ceiling into the middle of Partridge's Pharmacy and turned up in a hook at the end, on which the unshaded jet, lighted thus early, swung impaled. It hung there like a friendly, bogus serpent hissing against the literal *plunk* of water striking the paving stones outside, and it partly illumined the shop lined with reposeful rows of jars. It also revealed in part, the top part, Timothy himself in his mohair sack coat. His nether limbs in the great blot of shadow cast by the stove he sat hugging might have been those of fish, beast, or human for all the jet disclosed.

The sack coat, though it was Timothy's daily dress in the shop, hung with a vaguely accidental look from his narrow shoulders which managed to convey through the cloth a distinction deserving of more sumptuary covering. The light struck the back of his head bent over his reading; his hair, worn long, almost to his collar, was thick and stiff and of fine raven black. Hair, bones, and coat, taken together, suggested a naturally extravagant mind within severely clipped by the sharp blades of circumstance.

The pharmaceutical journal in his hand carried accounts of rare drugs, discoveries that gave promise of eliminating some of the ancient scourges of mankind, but the heartening news brought no elation to Timothy. He studied the price list and clucked, he glanced about the drowsing shop and shook his head, he thought of the numerous people who had calls on his generosity because they were poor or relatives or both, or because they had performed special services for the late Confederacy, still an actuality to the faithful in these lati-

4

tudes. Thus it was that the pharmacy ran on a shoe-string; besides, as his sister Penelope always said, "It's wrong to make money out of people's afflictions."

This saying of Penelope's came up through the page Timothy held and overlay the print. She was six years older than he, and her opinions had a way of following him about, of rearing up like a signpost when the road forked and gently pointing out the right way. Bustled along by her conviction, he usually found the right way easier to take than the primrose path; her rich, warm voice persuaded him to rightness; yet feeling her ardent and personable presence beside his rocking chair, he stirred, rattled his journal fretfully, and bethought him that he was chilly.

Through the isinglass panes in the fat paunch of the stove, he saw that the coals had indeed burned low. He opened the little door, decided against putting on more coal for the present, and blew a hopeful gust with the bellows. The embers obliged him by sending a red glow through the aperture. His legs, now withdrawn from the shadow, proved to be quite ordinary, thinnish legs and terminated in feet comfortably snubbed into carpet slippers. But the ruddy shaft slanting from below caught his face and shoulders in a half-satanic light. It threw into relief the mournful descending curve of his mustache; it reddened his oval jaw, and his eyes under his high shining forehead sent back into the depths an answering glare. Bent toward the opening, he seemed to be invoking the Pit.

After a while he closed the stove door and sat back,

5

relaxed in his rocker. He glanced idly toward the windows; seen under the weak and sallow gas jet, his face had nothing of Satan about it. It was the face of a good man, bewhiskered in the prevailing fashion, enjoying in the cosy cave of his shop an hour of unexpected quiet, vouchsafed him by the kind gods of the weather who were keeping people at home with this drumming rain. The rows and rows of bottles created a sense of order in life; in the front windows the great glass jars of green and amber liquid jeweled his surroundings at small expense. Beyond them the street was deep blue and empty, the color of space itself.

Suddenly Timothy caught a glimpse of a large black sphere flying past, as if a dark planet whirling on its course had shone for a moment in the reflected light from the shop window. It flashed again in the second window, but at the door it halted and pressed against the glass panes, collapsed to a narrow wedge, and on the instant the shop bell jangled as the door sprang open and a young woman stood inside the threshold. The long cloak thrown round her swept the rainy outdoors into the security of the shop. Water poured from the folds of her black cotton umbrella and ran in a tiny dark stream along the floor.

Timothy put on the spectacles he wore largely because of the magian dignity they lent him, and said, "Good evening, ma'am," in a voice from which ran a like trickle of surprise. As the girl stood and stared at him without speaking, he got up and went behind the counter, add-

6

ing, "Come in out of the wet—and close the door, *if* you please."

Without shifting her scrutiny of him she reached one hand behind her and swung the door to; the bell fastened to it jangled again as it slammed. Bad-mannered piece! said Timothy to himself. Utter want of consideration. . . . The girl's unfriendly eyes left him and went round the shop, searching it from the frieze of little Gothic arches that framed the top shelf to the heavy mortars and the big stone jars lined up on the floor. When she had finished her deliberate inventory she came up to the counter.

"I want a jar of solanum—a large jar."

Her voice was challenging, like the ring of a coin on the counter. Unsuitable, thought Timothy, who had old-fashioned views about women and soft speech—almost discordant.

"Have you the prescription?" Mechanically he adopted her abrupt address, thinking: Bad manners are as catching as measles.

She hesitated, then brought from under her cloak a crocheted purse, a cylinder of faded silk. She felt the lean mesh and shook her head. "I must have left it at home."

"Well . . . solanum is a pretty powerful drug," he said kindly. "I don't like to mix it without a physician's order."

"It's for my father—he has a bad earache. You don't need a prescription. And you surely can't expect me to go all the way home to get it—in this weather."

7

She stared through the shop window at the rain drenching off the eaves and making a thick silver fringe where the light caught it. Timothy took a good look at her over his glasses. She had never been in the shop, he was sure, nor could he remember having seen her about the town. But then he was not observant of people; he was a little nearsighted, he frowned down on the pavement when he walked; his thinking and his curiosity were bounded by the shop and his reading. So he might have passed her on the street—though she had a crispness about her you didn't easily forget. He suddenly saw that she was small; the long cloak and her commanding manner had given him a deceptive impression of height when she stood at the door. Damp ringlets straggled wispily from the scarf tied under her chin.

"There are several kinds of nightshade," he parried. "I can't be sure what your prescription calls for. Solanum Virginianum, solanum nigrum—"

"That's it."

He was used to mixing solanum in small quantities for earache, neuralgia, even to cure whitlows. But that headstrong manner of hers—

"My delivery-boy will be back after a while. You'd better let me send him to your house for the prescription. Do you live far from here?" He got out the slate on which he jotted his memoranda and prepared to write down the address, wondering if she had no relative, no servant to escort her through the streets at this time of night.

8

What irked Timothy most about his customer was her refusal to bear a responsible part in conversation. She answered you or not, as she pleased; and if she did speak, very likely it was without looking at you. He had a picture of what Sister Penny would think of such manners. There was a long pause now in which the gas jet resumed its cheerful hissing against the rain.

"It's late already," the girl said without turning her head. "The moon is rising—"

Timothy was sufficiently startled to glance from her profile to the streaming panes. The creature was daffy! "Come, now— You aren't going to pretend you see the moon in the window! It's pouring cats and dogs."

"Dogs—ugh! I hate them! But the moon is out, you know, above these black clouds . . . from the other side they look like miles and miles of puffed muslin. 'Trip, sing at moonrising: Waste, wane, sleep again . . .' "

As if it were a sort of rune she were repeating. And humming seemed to join in, like other voices far overhead.

Well, really—thought Timothy. What is this? The romantic talk of young ladies? Not likely. Mooniness didn't fit in with a personality so harsh and wild. A bluestocking, maybe, a besotted reader like himself, but of astronomy rather than alchemy—a taste for astronomy or physical geography might produce this beyond-the-clouds view of the world.

She suddenly dropped the runic manner and turned to look about the shop again, including Timothy in an amiable inventory. "You have a nice place here—I've

9

never been in before. What a pretty row of blue jars!"

The long shelf of little porcelain jars did indeed make a gay cerulean band across the dark wall of the shop. Timothy warmed quickly to her new tone of voice, which had somehow become personal. "They're English apothecary's ware, and quite old. They do look shiny and cheerful—as if they contained the cures for all the ills that plague people. But"—he heaved a mocking sigh— "I'm afraid that's a foolish pretension; as some doubter once remarked, more men die of the physic than of the disease."

This was not the proper thing to say to a customer, but then his hearer was hardly a proper customer. She had opened her cloak and begun to move, with a swing that was easy in spite of her bulky clothes, among the crucibles and glass cases cluttering the shop. Her dress, which covered her from neckline to shoe-top in the fashion of the period, left everything to the imagination and even stimulated that faculty, and Timothy became suddenly conscious of her body inside the bell-shape, of a simple and natural declaration it made of its presence, which flushed him with sensations at once lively and a little embarrassing. Her casual movement—or was anything about this siren quite casual?—described a circle that seemed to be narrowing on Timothy, when it brought her close to the shelf of blue jars. She paused and read the provocative labels with lazy interest: P. Canth.—P. Myrrh—Pulv. Aloes—P. Ipecac.

"What's that?" She pointed, unapologetically, to the shelf above Timothy's hand.

He turned and looked up. "This?" The clear glass jar held some small brown objects. "Just a frog and a pair of newts." He took them down and set them on the counter. "They're sort of interesting because they're not found locally. There used to be a journeyman apothecary who came through here; he sometimes sends me biological specimens from wherever his beat takes him."

The girl picked up the jar and turned it in her hand, fascinated, apparently, by the mummified creatures beginning to fall to powder.

"They should be in preservative, but it dried out a good while back. From my neglect," he added.

His disarming honesty brought the first spontaneous smile to her face, a look almost of liking. She set the jar on the counter. "And now can I have my solanum, please?"

There was nothing of coaxing or demanding in her manner. She made a polite and reasonable request, the kind to which Timothy was most susceptible.

She must have seen hesitancy in his face, for she exclaimed, "Wait—" and, searching some inside pocket, she held out a soiled paper. "I did bring it after all!"

Timothy opened it and read the prescription, though grease spots from many refillings and the slovenly Latin of an earlier day made it all but illegible. The blurred signature was unfamiliar; not a physician of this locality, nor, he suspected, of this century.

"Well, this is an old fellow," he temporized. "We call these ingredients by their modern names. I don't even know that I have them all—that long drought last

11

fall dried up the St. John's woods before the plants could be gathered, and shortened local supplies." He strolled along the shelves pretending to look while he thought how to meet the situation. The mixture prescribed was distinctly queer, he couldn't think what it was designed to cure; and it omitted the oily base— though that was not significant, many doctors allowed their patients some latitude in mixing medicines at home. Still, solanum was a drug to keep track of, and he didn't believe that story about the father's earache. He took down a jar or two and showed her that they were empty, as he knew they would be.

Perfunctorily he pulled out several wooden drawers containing roots of various sorts and shut them again, passing over, however, a drawer marked "corks" which contained other roots, purveyed mostly to poor whites and Negroes from the back door. In this he could actually have found a kind of nightshade, a horse nettle, popular as an aphrodisiac; serve her right if— But no, what he ought to sell her was a box of Beecham's Pills; undoubtedly she was liverish, with all those queer notions.

This gave him an idea. "Here's something that will be just right for you," he said, "just the ticket." He opened the glass case that held his line of patent medicines and took out a box of Swift's Specific. "Specific" in Timothy's observation meant exactly the opposite— good for everything, hence good for nothing. But at least she couldn't harm herself or anyone else with it. He read the label aloud. " 'Nature's own remedy, made

12

from roots gathered in Carolina by a recipe obtained
from a half-breed Cherokee . . .' Undoubtedly there are
several varieties of solanum in it. 'Cures cancer, catarrh,
eczema, ulcers, and blood-taint.' " Whatever ailed her,
that ought to cover it. "Take as much as you can put
on the point of a knife in a wineglassful of water—"

He swung around in the narrow passage and ran full
tilt into the girl, who had come soundlessly behind the
counter and stood at his back. Her light eyes, close to
his, struck through him with such a look of determina-
tion and power that Timothy involuntarily fell back a
step or two. The natural impulse to beg her pardon rose
to his lips and froze there; naked intensity of this kind
would have no use for apologies.

"You have the solanum and you might just as well
give it to me. I can tell what you've got in those jars and
drawers—it takes more than glass and wood to hide things
from me. And your mind, Doctor, is even easier to see
through. One believer smells out another fast enough."

Timothy retreated in wild confusion, because he
didn't care to sort out his motley beliefs, and her
unshrinking gaze pushed him toward the horrid abysm
of logic. She went on. "It's time we dropped the pre-
tence. This is the night for a meeting; I'm short the
necessities—the drought has pinched other folks beside
you—and I have to come here for them. So don't waste
any more time with this flapdoodle."

The word was like a slap in the face. What kind of
were-woman this was, bursting into his shop with her
talk of meetings and ointments, he couldn't decide. Was

13

she real or sham? But he felt disinclined to find out by thwarting her. . . .

Cautiously he brought the ingredients together and began to pound them in a mortar.

He took his time, because a queer sensation was growing on him of being dragged from his moorings. The mixture burned his fingers a little, his body felt light. The girl stood stock-still where he had left her; he would have liked to tell her to go back to that part of the shop where customers properly belonged, but he saved his breath. When he had prepared the components he went through the back room of the house to the pantry, where he took a small firkin of lard from Sister Penny's cold shelf and brought it back to the prescription counter. Meantime his visitor had returned of her own accord to the front of the store and stood looking moodily out of the window.

He carefully measured out the lard, mixed it with the ingredients, and solemnly pasted the label on the jar: *Apply twice daily for earache.* Then he went behind the front counter and wrapped it up. "This is for external use only," he said. "Solanum should be mixed with an equal quantity of pure hog's lard before applying, so I took the precaution of mixing it for you. This will make it useless for anything but an external anesthetic."

He half-expected another outburst, but she gave him a sharp, surprising smile. "That's all right—it's no good to me without a grease base. You could have saved your lard, high as it is now. How much do I owe you?"

"Oh—about thirty-five cents," he said, remembering the lean mesh purse.

She opened it, took out a fifty-cent piece, and snapped it down on the counter. "What you've given me is cheap at fifty cents. Good night, Dr. Partridge." Snatching up the jar, she made for the door.

"Wait a moment!" He wanted to draw her out further about those queer ideas of hers, but his words were lost in the shrilling of the bell as she jerked the door open. She took off from the threshold like a night bird swooping, a darkness on the dark.

A harsh squeaking came in and filled the quiet shop; the great mortar and pestle that hung above the entrance were shaking on their metal bracket from some passing gust. The cold, damp draft struck Timothy to the bone. He went over and slammed the door himself.

"Whew!" he said, sitting down on the edge of his chair, for the strong dream-sensation began to fade and left a slight dizziness, more of the limbs than of the head. "A queer creature, and no mistake. . . ." He went on muttering platitudes to cover the unsettling fact that he really didn't know what to think about his visitor. To make it further confusing, the visitation seemed more dreamlike the more he himself withdrew from the dream-area and his senses picked up again his area of reality—his apothecary's scales on the counter, the small-talk of the gas jet, the smell of orris root and spirits of nitre.

The entrance of the delivery-boy hastened Timothy's

return to normal. The boy was soaked to the skin; he stood at the back door of the shop and shimmered darkly like a small sea monster floated up by the rain. Timothy interrogated him about his errands and received answers not much more satisfactory than he would have had from a rather bright fish. Pollo was a *boulevardier* from the heart, he sought the sidewalks even in a downpour; but he came of a colored family who were pensioners of Penelope's and he had to be given a job regardless of his weak sense of direction and of his creative lying to disguise his truancies. Timothy satisfied himself that no serious errors had been made and told the boy to go home and dry his clothes, he doubted if any other customers would come in this rainy evening.

No sooner had Pollo dived out of the door than a violent agitation of the bell mocked at this judgment. Timothy glanced up nervously, but it was only Dr. Golightly, whose violence was unpremeditated, the result of energy and bulk. "Howdy, old poisoner!" he cried, and all the glass vials and shelf bottles gave a faintly startled chime. "Fine weather for ducks, eh? But I s'pose you don't put your nose outdoors on a day like this. You just hole up and mix potions to kill customers off with."

"Maybe I do at that." Timothy smiled guiltily. "But I'll bet a hat you shuffle more people off to the graveyard than I do. Come in—come in, and shut that door. There ought to be a special cold shelf in Hell for people who leave doors open behind them."

16

Golightly came in and banged the door. He seemed to trample the floor under with his big India-rubber boots. He threw his satchel on the counter and went over to the stove, opening the wide cape of his checked wool greatcoat. "It's like a cold shelf in Hell right here," he complained. He put one foot on the base of the stove and spread his red, gloveless hands. "You're the stingiest damn fellow with your fuel, Tim."

"When your coal is low in the bin, you're apt to be stingy with it," said Timothy dryly. "You don't think I relish being chilly, do you?" He came and joined the doctor by the stove.

"Hell and death! I never skimp food on my table nor fire in my stove. The locomotive can't run without steam." He opened the isinglass door and spat extravagantly on the coals.

The fire had sunk in the past half hour and the shaft that caught Golightly's face produced no satanic transformation, it merely caricatured the full, ruddy flesh, the terrier eyebrows that were his already, and rendered his little boast superfluous. It tipped with light the gray bristles coming out of his ears and nose like spears glistening in an ambush.

Timothy was not really offended by these bluff comments, though they put him on the defensive. "That's mighty handsome talk," he argued, "but my business doesn't allow for overeating. This is a poor community —we've had a war, and a peace that's almost as bad as a war. Sister Penny and I can't indulge ourselves in the matter of food and warmth when so many of our neighbors are cold and hungry. Not as long as we profess Christianity." He pulled his mustachios with thumbs and forefingers to a sharper, a more pious point. "Of course ordinary Christianity would do well enough for me," he added parenthetically, "but Sister professes a fancy brand, and that takes upkeep."

Golightly filled his lungs and gave a great porpoise-snort that sent the raindrops flying off his coat. He couldn't talk down Christianity, and when he couldn't talk you down, he snorted like a porpoise. "Listen, brother, I 'tend a God's plenty of free patients—enough to guarantee me a toehold in Christendom—but I keep the engine stoked. And who operates this pharmacy anyway, Penny or you?"

"I operate it," said Timothy sulkily. He put his foot on the opposite side of the iron base, keeping the sturdy stove between them while he parried his adversary's downright thrusts. "But Sister Penny is a very unusual person—she can't help being generous, she bubbles with the milk of human kindness. She has a woman's sympathy for suffering."

"Suffering and bubbling be damned! What is she, a Jersey cow? I know she's kind, of course she is! And I honor her for it. I come on her tracks all the time in my practice, supplying patients with medicine free of charge. But at whose expense, eh? She ought to try her woman's sympathy once on running a pharmacy, or any business where you have to make a ledger balance—"

While Timothy let Golightly talk himself out he followed his own thoughts for a little, speculating on

18

the antagonism between his sister and his friend. Will is bighearted as all outdoors, he would say (for he was always defending each to the other), and Penny would smile indulgently and answer, I know he does a great deal of good—and he has the finest set of whiskers in Charleston. But she wouldn't have him for her doctor, although he was a cousin and it was quite pointed for her to have Dr. Porter, who was a good doctor but no kin at all. Will, she said, had a very materialistic outlook, and she couldn't stand his keeping his hunting dogs in his office.

Many of Will's patients found it trying, when they went to have a boil lanced or their tonsils out, to hear the hounds sniffing round; they grumbled in private about the doggy smell thickening the air, the hairs on the shabby upholstery, the fleas in summer. But Penny was the only one with the hardihood to stand up to the popular physician about his pets—they had had several memorable encounters about it. Yet it was more than dogs in offices that set them against each other. . . .

Timothy came up with a splash into the freshet of Golightly's argument. ". . . and of course we're poor down here—we're poor as rats!" He laughed spontaneously, belittling the curse that weighed on the half-prostrate South. "Well, what you gonna do about it? Get rich, that's what I say. Get busy and make some money."

"You tell me how to do it. And there are still moss-backs, you know, who cling to the old-fashioned idea that money isn't the answer to everything."

19

"Money! That poor pariah," Golightly cried flamboyantly. "Everybody cusses money—the root of all evil —Devil's get! But secretly everybody wants it, it's the illicit love of all men—and most women—"

Uttering this heresy, the doctor took his foot off the stove, stamped up and down, and flapped his cape. The Flying Pill-Roller, people called him, seeing him dash through the streets, the buggy-top folded back, the full cape streaming out behind like fashionable plaid wings.

To escape being run over, Timothy dodged from under the wheels of this headlong argument. "By the way, there's something I want to ask you. Just now I had a most singular visitor—a young lady who came in wanting solanum. It appears she has a father who is subject to earache—maybe from having to listen to her. I can't place her, somehow; she wasn't pretty exactly, and she's sort of small and harsh, no gloves and no manners either. She had the most extraordinary eyes; they can singe you like a chemical—I still feel as if I had some kind of phosphorus burn from her being here."

"My God, Tim!" Golightly turned a diagnostic stare on his cousin. "You must be seeing apparitions. What color were these singular eyes?"

Timothy pulled his chin and thought a while. "I can't remember. And they don't burn all the time, thank God, or I'd be a pile of cinders. I do recollect her eyebrows though; they were dark, too thick for beauty, and rounded. My physiognomy books say high-arched eyebrows are a sign of courage—"

20

"Pshaw! An extraordinary critter, I must say. How old was she?"

Timothy thought again. "You know, I'd find it pretty hard to say. Youngish looking. But she seemed quite mature. Or perhaps she's just wicked . . . bad people have a disconcerting way of seeming more knowledgeable than good people. She had on a long, dark cloak, like a man's—a hand-me-down, I imagine. I'd give a lot to know what her name is, where she lives, and so on."

"Why the Devil didn't you ask her?"

"She wasn't the sort of person you ask questions of —unessential questions, that is. She has a way of chopping off with a look any excrescences in your conversation."

"I can't think of anybody that fits such a fanciful description . . . unless it might be one of Charley Farr's girls. You know him? He lives over by the jail and has a big litter of daughters. They say the youngest one is wild and unruly. I've seen her scuttling along the street, but I can't say she ever swinged me like phosphorus. Do you feel bilious? You better take two grains of calomel."

Timothy had studious refined features, the kind that could go obstinate as a lightwood knot. "You should have been here, then you'd know what I mean. She was going to get that solanum if it killed her, or rather if it killed me. And somehow her story about the father's having an earache didn't ring true. I suspect she's up to no good. The prescription she had was an antique and by a doctor I never heard of—some foreigner, from his name."

"Well, Charley Farr, if that's whose daughter she is, could have earache, backache, or bellyache the way he lays aboard demon rum."

"She may not even be his daughter; but whoever begat her, I wouldn't want her hanging round me with that solanum."

"It's strong stuff—strong stuff," Golightly agreed. "You have to ride it with a light hand on the bit. I've given one grain internally for some nervous affections, and with good success. But a dense alkaloid like that is unhealthy to fool with unless you know how to use it. Externally, now, it's a different kettle of fish; for dilating the pupils I like it better in some ways than belladonna—"

Timothy began to walk around the shop, his chilly hands in his pockets. "I have some books," he muttered, "that give the ingredients for witches' brews; those creatures love nightshade, you know, and aconite, mixed with all kinds of vile messes. It wouldn't surprise me . . . there are a lot of queer people loose in this town."

The doctor drew his overhanging eyebrows together and looked out sharply from under them. "Fiddlesticks! You spend too much time messing with books and herbs. You ought to throw out those roots you hide under the counter and peddle from the back door. A good pharmacist has no business fooling with that kind of tripe. The trouble with mumbo jumbo is, it's a boomerang, it witches you in the end."

"What do you mean by mumbo jumbo? Don't we all

deal with something of the kind? Take this stuff you prescribe and I sell—Bosanko's Cough and Lung Syrup" —Timothy opened a glass case and took up some bottles —"Bradfield's Female Regulator—do they do any good except by mumbo jumbo? And even the drugs you would call scientific medicine . . . you say solanum is a poison, but do you know why a dense alkaloid should be poisonous to man? All physic works by magic of a kind."

Golightly slammed the door of a cupboard he had been prying into and there was the sharp *ting* of colliding glass. "Magic? Pshaw! Seeing is believing, that's what I say." He turned on Timothy. "Why don't you go North, man—sell out this ratty little business of yours and take the money to go away. Get some new ideas— study modern pharmacy—work in a drug manufactory! Go to New York, or Boston! Your guts are squeezed here. Why, you even look like a bed-slat."

Deeply affronted, Timothy drew himself up taller, which was not a happy move. His narrow shoulders and hips, the stiff verticals of his trouser legs, did give him the appearance of having been accidentally elongated in the pliable time of infancy. "Not me—I'm an unreconstructed provincial. What have they got up there that we haven't except money and machines? They're too rich for my blood; and a pricking of my thumbs tells me those machines will carry us all to Hell someday. You don't go North, I notice," he went on, "though you uphold their materialism and pretend to admire their manufactories and their great railroads."

"That's so, but, in spite of my 'materialism,' I'm not ambitious to get rich. If I can keep out of the clutches of the pawnbrokers, own a piece of land and some houn' dogs, give my family three square meals a day and a few tomfooleries—everybody ought to have a few tomfooleries—I'm content with my lot. I love this Low-Country of ours and couldn't breathe away from it. But you are different—you've let defeat suck you dry."

The bare idea of putting out from his riparian safety so agitated Timothy that he said nothing and let Golightly rush on.

"God Almighty, man, we got to heave out of the bog sometime! I recollect well the last campaigns when drugs were pitifully short—I've used every damn kind of stinking weed and plant trying to find substitutes for physic cut off by the Yankee blockade—and lucky for us that the Southern woods are rich in medicinal herbs. But that was a long time ago, and surgical instruments don't sprout in the woods, manufactories have to sprout first, we need more fruit like glass and steel—thank God there's a Democrat in the White House at last and business in the South ought to be looking up."

Golightly's war record had become legendary in this section, but Timothy had a way of forgetting it. He himself had been only ten when the war began, and he still felt inadequate that he hadn't managed his birth better, hadn't come along in time to bear a part in that holy cause. He was seldom aware of the ten years' difference in their ages; in so many ways his boisterous cousin seemed younger, or perhaps, Timothy thought, he himself had grown old before his time. . . .

Nevertheless, his blood was up now and he had one shot left in his musket. He leaned on the counter and took aim.

"Maybe I'd have more money to put into my business if I could bring myself to gamble in Wall Street."

He had the satisfaction of seeing Golightly teeter, rocked back a little in his India rubbers. "Gamble, eh?" he snorted. "The Deuce and all! Life is a gamble! Every day is a gamble—if you're alive, that is. And as to Wall Street, why not bring some of that Yankee money into the South? 'If you can't beat 'em, jine 'em'—that's what I say."

"If you can 'jine' 'em," said Timothy meanly. "If you're sharp enough." For you could always tell: Will shot badly and cursed more eloquently when one of his "fliers" had dropped him with a grinding thud. But on the other hand his successes brought him many little luxuries, such as the sporty checked coat.

"I have heavy responsibilities to carry," Timothy continued primly. "I can't take that kind of risk, with two older people to support."

"You could carry them better if you had a good business!" cried Will. "How can you make money if you freeze your customers and have nothing to sell them? But I haven't got any more time to waste. I just dropped by for some vaseline and powdered alum— I s'pose you still keep *them* in this flat-bottomed pharmacy. There'll be plenty of sore throats and rheumatic fever after this rain, blast it, and I won't get away to go deer-hunting Saturday." As Timothy put the required articles glumly on the counter, Golightly picked them up and threw them into his satchel. "My patients love to get their feet wet on Thursdays, I've noticed, just in time to come down with grippe Saturdays and keep me in town." He snapped the satchel shut. "Well, so long. Better take my advice and get out of this 'gator hole of yours." Muffling himself in his cape, he made for the door.

Timothy glanced involuntarily at the floor-boards, expecting to see them ground to splinters by Will's big feet. When the dust had settled he walked about, angrily putting the shop to rights. What an evening! He felt all stirred up inside; these two encounters were giving him dyspepsia. He went to the sink and took a teaspoonful of soda in half a glass of water.

Returning the jars and bottles from the counter to the shelves, he halted a moment in surprise. The glass jar holding the frogs and newts was gone. He looked quickly about; its place on the shelf gaped dark. The determined face of the strange girl came up before him; but would even such queer tastes as hers have prompted her to hide a jar of moldering frogs under her cloak? Maybe Will had gathered them up by mistake and chucked them into his satchel. Pondering this riddle, he went across the hall to his cluttered bedroom behind the shop.

Penelope had had the carved walnut bookcases containing his uncle's library of science and esoterica

26

moved into this room as the best means of getting rid of them, and the dry-fruited cornices, the rows of calf-bound books, paneled it around with heavy brownness. Timothy himself kept piled on every chair and table and in every corner the magazines, pamphlets, old news-papers he had collected, apparently in the assurance that he would one day do something terrific with all that knowledge. The brownness and muddle, how-ever, well satisfied his esthetic tastes. The books stand-ing close-packed on the shelves both soothed and ex-cited him; the pamphlets and clippings . . . in all his nights of reading he had never gone half way through these pages that closed round him like a brambly thicket. He stepped out of his low-quarter shoes—which remained by the hearth neatly teamed, ready to proceed when his ghostly part, having enough of waywardness, should require sole-leather again—and began to open the glass doors of the cases, going to and fro over the carpet in his stocking feet and pulling out books which Penelope had luckily never concerned herself to open.

A treatise on the Manichaeans engaged him for a while. The theory that the Devil is coequal with God struck him forcibly; it would explain lots of strange things about life. For one thing, it would explain why he so sincerely admired his elder sister's goodness and generosity, but had so many temptations toward wicked-ness and materialism himself. Not that his wickedness took an active form—it went on mostly in his heart, but that, as Satan well knew, was the worst kind.

But he put the question of Good and Evil aside for

a while and continued his search along the dark alley that ran through the back of his mind. He leafed through an ancient almanac in pursuit of a recipe for mixing herbs and simples; the item eluded him, but he was rewarded by an even more arresting one—a prophecy that 1886 was a year in which great mischief was to be wrought. Readily flattered by such signal attentions to a present which was his, he turned the page down and laid the booklet on a handy pile for future reference.

His energetic burrowings, however, quickly covered it with others; reminded of his trade, he dipped into a monograph on the cryptogamic plants of the United States and willingly devoted half an hour to improving his knowledge of the place of fungi in the economy of the world. Besides, he enjoyed thinking about blights, molds, mildews, and the toxic principle of poisonous mushrooms. These last, he read, "depend on their power to coagulate the albumen of the blood and thus arrest the circulation." Pure magic! But whether of God or the Devil he couldn't determine for the moment.

It was late in the night when he came on what he wanted, the *Discouerie of Witchcraft* by an old Scot. Carefully holding the volume with its broken hinges, he took it over to the fireplace and held it up to the jet beside the mantel. Its yellowing pages rewarded him with sundry directions for witches' brews which he read with an apothecary's careful observation: aconite or wolfsbane mixed with soot, the blood of a bat—yes, and solanum nigrum, all seethed with the fat of young children in a copper cauldron. And what a diversity of creatures dealt familiarly with these prescriptions! Seeing is believing, but believing is also seeing, and by the spectacles of faith Timothy easily bested nearsighted reason. The bookcases, the shabby carpet, dissolved around him while he slid along the sharply tilted plane of the changelings, incubi, hags, and hobgoblins.

With these he visualized quite clearly a dark face capped with a tall headdress, bending over his past. Maum Rachel, his old nurse, was said to have second sight, and certainly she had succeeded in making real to his youthful eyes the spirits of the countryside, the ghost-dogs and witch doctors, the mysterious, the enchanting, the unpredictable creatures who lent richness and murk to the earth she trod. . . . Maum Rachel was no spirit; she still lived in the country, to which she had returned to spend her old age, but her strong personality often invaded Timothy's mind like a visitation.

He remembered her taking him once to see a cousin of hers, a gaunt Negro known as West Indie, who had come to the States on a visit and who had reduced Maum Rachel no less than himself to a condition of near-hysteria with his tales of dead men called zombies on his island, corpses that could be brought back to the image of life and made to work for those who knew the spell; of fire-hags who could be sent through an enemy's cane-fields at night to set them ablaze. It had seemed to Timothy then that some blood kinship existed between West Indie's creatures and Maum Rachel's, a connection no queerer, and no less actual, than that of the stranger with his Creole accent and Maum Rachel herself. Now this problem of consanguinity enthralled him; he began to find correspondences between these tutelary beings of his childhood and the black, white, and red spirits of the Scottish writer, which gave the whole supernatural world a character vaster, more massive, and at the same time more familiar. He returned to his book and read tale after tale of the miraculous transportation of witches, of demons and sylvans up to the old tricks, thinking that they were like second cousins once removed whose conduct you might not care for but whom you would never really fear. How steeped the Scottish ground, the English hills, in the Celtic spirit . . . a desire took him by the throat to go away, not to the ugly brick drug factories, but to England where the lost wisdom lay like gold in the earth to be dug by the faithful, the curious, the seeker after answers.

Timothy wriggled his cold toes and laid the book down on the nearest pile of papers. He got up and strolled into the shop. The stove had gone out; but a stale warmth lingered and brought him a little comfort as he tidied up for the next day. Putting up the heavy iron bar across the front door, he noticed a queer smell in the air; he looked about and discovered by the sink the mortar in which he had mixed the solanum ointment. He picked up the pestle and sniffed the not unpleasant turpentinish smell. A salve for the miraculous transportation of witches, eh? He laughed silently, thinking how he must have clogged their wings by substituting the fat of swine for the fat of infants. Or had he?

With a spatula he scraped out the residue sticking to the sides of the mortar and, putting it into a small crock, covered it closely. Now, to find a safe place to hide it from the meddlings of his apprentice and Pollo— A dark corner behind the jar of Epsom salts proved just the spot, and he tucked it away for further study when the shop should be warmer.

When he awoke next day it was still raining. He opened the windows in the shop, lighted the stove, and finished dressing by it. Then he sat down and read his daily passage in the Bible. His researches of the evening before remained safely in the world to which they belonged, so he felt no contradiction in this act. If you finished the evening in the company of Evil, you should begin the day in the company of Good; it was only a sensible precaution. By accident or natural proclivity he opened at First Samuel, and reading about the visit of the doomed Saul to the great witch by the fountain of En-dor, he felt a prickling in all his sensitive length as his nimble imagination and the fervor of his belief raised spirits from the cramped print.

That evening when Timothy went to his room to get ready for supper he noticed a tear in his coat; the mohair had shredded and pulled out at the armhole. He gave a cluck of annoyance but hurried on with his dressing because the room was as cold as charity and

31

because it was nearly seven o'clock, the hour at which they "took tea." As he stood at the washstand soaping his hands he could hear Penelope in the pantry behind his room putting the tray on the dumb-waiter. Shivering, he slipped into a serge coat and, throwing the other over his arm for her to mend, he went into the hall and climbed one flight to the dining room at the front over the shop.

In this room the fire was kept up all day. As hungry for warmth and light as for food, Timothy closed the door behind him and went over to the hearth. The third occupant of the house was reading his paper by the yellow-globed lamp on the center table; he sat so stiffly in his high-backed chair that only his eyes moving under their lids broke up the image of death, but he said "good evening" politely as Timothy came into his range of vision. Mr. Dombie had been brought to the Partridge house in the last year of the War to recover from his wounds, and had stayed twenty-one years; after their parents' death the sister and brother had not even suggested another arrangement—indeed Penelope, who had nursed him back to life, still regarded the care of the homeless man as her most sacred obligation.

A bell tinkled below-stairs which was Timothy's signal to haul up the dumb-waiter, so he crossed the hall and went through Mr. Dombie's bedroom above his own, and into a small room at the back. He pulled on the ropes in the shaft and soon the tea tray rose out of the black depths with the teapot like a setting hen

in its wadded cosy, the teacups and covered dishes surrounding it in a fat flock.

As Timothy, carrying the tray, reached the dining-
room door, Penelope came up the stairs to open it for
him. From long practice they had come to time this
maneuver exactly to save Mr. Dombie from having to
stir his crippled legs. Holding the door ajar, Penelope,
who was half a head taller, looked down on Timothy
and the tray with maternal searching; apparently they
both passed muster, because an affectionate smile
softened her strongly cast features. At one end of the
dinner table a white tea cloth had been laid on top of
the green velours cover, and on this Timothy set the
tray.

"Tea is ready—will you come to table, Mr. Dombie?"
said Penelope, taking off the tea cosy and beginning
to pour.

Mr. Dombie after a pause laid down his paper; his
reply came diffidently, as if some dusty substance
clogged his throat.

"Why, thank you, Miss Penny, I believe I will." All
these years of living under the same roof had not broken
down the formality of their address to each other.
Timothy helped him to a chair near Penelope's and
they sat down together at that end of the table.

Penelope passed the biscuits, the cold stew left from
their midday dinner, and some pumpkin preserves.
Timothy tasted his stew and put his fork down with
momentary irritation. Mr. Dombie was forbidden to eat

33

salt and sometimes Penelope, who prepared all his food separately with her own hands, made the rest of the household finish up his special dishes, a frugality that never failed to irk Timothy. Not that the lack was hard to supply, and without speaking he went to the sideboard and brought back the saltcellar. As he sprinkled his plate elaborately Penelope glanced at him under her large lids, but she too refrained from comment; by only the slightest motions they carried on the argument their discipline seldom allowed to break into words. Why should I be made to eat pap? Timothy's fork thumped out on the plate. And by the flutter of an eyelash, a disturbed motion of the hand, Penelope answered, You are unreasonable—and you think too much about food. . . .

While they ate she spread over the table like another cloth the pattern of the day's activities. The cook had left the kitchen dirty again when she went home after dinner. She really ought to be turned off; she'd never learn to be tidy and Penelope had stood all she could. The two men listened unresponsively and ate their supper because they found food more gratifying and because they had heard this before. Penelope had rescued the woman from some long-forgotten tribulation and was bound to her by her own benevolence in a slavery from which neither really desired manumission.

Unabashed, Penelope turned to more general subjects. She had gone that afternoon to a board meeting of an orphanage that was one of her fighting causes, and the treasurer had tried to thwart her schemes for improving certain unfortunate conditions.

"Why is it that treasurers—men treasurers"—she glanced with smiling reproach from Mr. Dombie to Timothy—"are so feeble in imagination? It's perfectly obvious that education is the South's most burning problem. We can get along without luxuries—in fact, we're better off without them—but good schooling for these children born since the War is a *necessity,* our whole future depends on it. But to every suggestion I made, that dull little man simply kept saying we had no funds for expansion. Well, I say we must give the children better teachers and better food—we can't afford *not* to— and the funds will be forthcoming. I put him to rout, I think; I got a resolution through . . ."

Under his irritation Timothy couldn't help being stirred by the gust of Penelope's confidence and conviction which blew people along, even male treasurers, their umbrellas turned inside out. She went on, "After all, which is more important, money or education?"

"Education, of course," said Mr. Dombie obligingly, setting down his cup and sucking the tea from the ends of his mustache. But Timothy said nothing because he thought Sister Penny was right but illogical, and he had never learned how to meet this dilemma effectively. He met it this time by a jerky movement that upset the saltcellar. "Clumsy!" she exclaimed, but her broad forehead and fine eyes turned on him indulgently and she smiled. Timothy drew a cross with his finger in the white pile on the table between them, but Penelope

35

ignored his look inviting her to do the same; she declined to placate the dark gods who breed quarrels—so he threw a pinch over his shoulder for good measure.

Penelope continued to provide the conversation; sitting at the head of the table, she was the dispenser to her household, of food, of comfort, and of ideas. And she did it with warmth and style. Her fresh coloring, her animation, offset the austerity of her dark hair, parted in the middle and piled flat on top of her head, leaving her ears nakedly exposed.

When the meal was finished Timothy carried the tray back to the dumb-waiter, Penelope removed the cloth and went down to the kitchen to wash the tea things. He returned to the dining room, which was also their sitting room; Mr. Dombie was in his armchair again, and Timothy sat down in its twin on the other side of the hearth to warm his cold feet, a complaint that afflicted him chronically.

Outdoors the rain had slackened to a cold quiet dripping which merely sealed in the warmth of the room. Mr. Dombie talked seldom and that was a comfort. The two men steeped in a cottony silence. The light, Timothy noticed with a sudden awareness of familiar things, suffused wood and chenille with a kind of luxuriance; the gas jets on either side the mantel wavered in their milky shades; the globe of the kerosene lamp shone like a little sun domesticated in the center of the table. Light itself, he thought, had been captured and enclosed in Penelope's service.

She came back presently and Timothy gave her his

36

place by the fire. She turned the gas jets lower, reaching up with a gesture that made the petty economy seem an evidence of seriousness and character, like the plain black dresses she habitually wore. Then she sat down with her sewing basket and Timothy took his allotted seat beyond hers. It was a straight chair that made few concessions to tired muscles, but obviously age and sex qualified Penelope and Mr. Dombie for possession of the two horsehair-covered armchairs on either side of the hearth.

The grate threw out a lovely arc of warmth, but beyond it lay an arc of chilliness which even the thick curtains could not temper. Cold little airs fingered Timothy's spine and added to his irritation. Furthermore he had forgotten to bring the book he was reading, and not for worlds would he plunge into the cold regions below to get it.

The sitting room offered a reader only the family Bible on the whatnot, a gift edition of *The Lay of the Last Minstrel* bound in the Scott tartan, and a photograph album of dead Partridges handsomely laid away in maroon plush. Timothy's mind thus lay open to the temptations Satan finds for the idle. He tilted his chair back and picked his teeth, then he put his hands for warmth into his trouser pockets and gazed about the room. In the surrounding air he discovered another area of chill than the one at his back, a picture of *The Last Judgment* on the wall in a corner. This painting with its message of impending doom had hung heavily over his childish head, especially in the War years, but

37

Papa considered it a salutary reminder of the briefness of mortality and, later, Penelope had kept it there because it was a copy of the work of a great Flemish artist. Familiarity had long since shrouded it from Timothy's sight; but now it came out of its cerements and gave him a fresh sensation. Below the central figure of Christ enthroned, the earth cracked to disgorge the dead (in a distressing state of nakedness), who were being seized and sorted into the Saved and the Damned. Two exophthalmic angels hustled the former toward Heaven while the sinners were being thrust into a horrid pit.

The naturalism with which the Flemish master had treated his fantasy suited Timothy's tastes exactly. He admired the lifelike figures and began to find resemblances in them—that knock-kneed fellow with the crutch was Mr. Dombie being helped toward the pearly gates, the handsome virago bound the other way was Sister Penny, giving the devils a bad time as she protested her fate and her bare condition. He glanced slyly at the two bent heads before him and his lips went up at the corners in their characteristic curve, then he returned to the picture to look for Will and his wife, Anna Maria. . . .

The childish fancy faded out. Mr. Dombie had begun to read from the newspaper about Queen Victoria's Golden Jubilee which was being prepared for next year, and Timothy's thoughts became meshed in the hypnotic singsong. . . . The day Penelope had brought the young stranger into the house throbbed dully in

Timothy's memory like a foreign body still encysted there. Fascinated and horrified, drawn and repelled, he had shrunk under the staircase as the stretcher passed by, all blood, bandages, and a dead man's face . . . and on that day his father had told him the undreamed-of, the impossible news that the South was going to lose the War. As to Mr. Dombie, Penny had nursed him back to life with fanatical care; passionate, wholehearted Penny . . . when the surgeons had laid him aside in the heavy rush of casualties, in the dreadful shortage of nurses and drugs, to make room for men who might be patched up and returned to the lines, Penny had refused to give him up, she had revolted against that cruel abandonment, she had brought him home and saved him.

How much she had saved in so doing might be open to question, for all Penny's care could not rebuild the nerves, the tissues, the bones splintered in the last desperate fight at Secessionville. Bleached, almost helpless, he seemed to have caught the shell fragments in his spirit too, as if the vital flow of life had only half returned to the vacant dwelling.

Thus it had befallen, Timothy saw, enlightened, as if the wick had been turned up in the lamp, that Mr. Dombie had become the slave of Penelope's devotion. But how had he himself succumbed—he who had inherited the fine constitution of the Partridges? A sharper, more insistent chill went through him. The love-slaves . . . a fanciful epithet; neither of them looked the part exactly. Yet neither of them stirred, he thought, without a ghostly silver clank around the ankles.

Timothy came to, acutely conscious of his twenty-six vertebrae against the narrow chair-back. He bethought him of his torn coat, and, when the nasal voice trailed off for a moment, he got up and took it to Penelope.

"Look at this sleeve, Sister; it's frayed out at the seam— Can I trouble you to mend it for me? It's almost new, this coat, I bought it only—let me see—winter before last, I think it was, but the seam has pulled already."

Penelope took it from him and clucked sympathetically. "I'll have to patch it, I'm afraid. All the materials we get these days are wretched. When I remember the fine alpacas Mama used to buy— This feels as if it were made of straw."

"I got this at Robinson's, so it should be a good coat. But I suspect Mr. Robinson puts out old dry goods sometimes. These threads are rotten; it's downright dishonest to sell a coat with no more wear in it than this."

Mr. Dombie lowered his paper. "Robinson was a good cavalry officer," he put in mildly. "He rode like a demon, until he was captured in Virginia."

Timothy was nettled. He should have sympathized with Mr. Robinson's difficulties in keeping his goods in stock but he didn't; he took a reprehensible satisfaction in blaming Mr. Robinson. "He may ride like a demon but he runs a miserable dry goods store. You can't build up a business unless you have good stock to sell. After all, you have to put out money before you can make money."

"Making money is not the most important thing in life," Penelope said.

There was something familiar to Timothy's ears about this exchange; familiar, yet curiously tangled. Penelope gave Mr. Dombie a protective glance that ranged her on his side and went on. "You oughtn't to say such things about Mr. Robinson, Timothy. I don't believe he would sell decayed material—he was in Hampton's Cavalry during the War. You must have sat in the east wind. That will sometimes loosen the fibers of cloth, they say."

"That's true," said Mr. Dombie, his thin face almost animated. "It must have been the east wind, Miss Penny. It's a mean wind, the east wind; you notice fish won't bite when it blows, fishing lines rot out, and it makes a man's wounds ache like the Old Boy."

From long discipline or sheer discouragement Timothy forbore to point out the non sequiturs in this conversation. He returned to his chair and, tilted back at a reckless angle, nursed his grievances for a while. Mr. Dombie's flat, persistent voice went on, reading a description of the Crystal Palace, and the glittering structure began to take shape in the small stuffy room. A craving seized Timothy to escape from the damaged structures of defeat and to see this brave palace reared on foreign ground. The English names woke in him a queer response, a desire that had throbbed lately.

He brought the forelegs of his chair down with a thump. "Sister, there's something I want to talk to you about. I'm thinking of going away."

41

It came on him with a certain surprise that under the thick coat of habitual yielding he still had a residue of spunk . . . perhaps one always has more than one knows.

The two faces by the fire turned on him in utter disbelief.

"I want to visit the Crystal Palace."

He felt as if the chair were still rocking under him in a precarious balance and went on quickly. "Besides, business is going badly—trade is falling off. Without any capital I haven't much chance of building it up."

"Why, Timothy, you astound me—" The remark was unnecessary; Penelope's rigidity, her fixed blue glance, spoke for her. "I had no idea you were worried about the shop. Why didn't you tell me?"

Timothy took a great gulp of breath to bolster himself. "Well, you know the shelves are half empty. And you know the income isn't enough to give us a decent living and support the charities you're interested in. What small profits the shop brings in go for these instead of being put back in the business."

"We live quite decently, I think." The color rose in Penny's cheeks. "And would you be willing to let the people suffer whom we are able to help—would you cut them off in order to put that money into the business?"

"Well, no," said Timothy fidgeting on his chair, a branch tossed by contrary winds. "But that's why I'm resolved to give up the shop, at least temporarily. Let someone buy it out who has the capital to make it a good one. Besides, the truth is, I need to brush up a bit; modern pharmacy is making great strides and leaving me behind. I need to go away and get some new ideas. With the proceeds from selling the business I'd like to go to London and study—" He spoke in a confident, even a grand manner.

There was silence for a few moments while Penelope sewed a little ostentatiously on Timothy's coat. Against the lamp her dark outline flowed from her crown of hair to the worn carpet, statuesque and profoundly mysterious. He didn't really know her, Timothy thought, staggered; after all the days of all those years in the same house. . . . His eye supplied the details the shadow subdued, the smooth grain of her hair like a fine red-brown wood, the generous curve of ear and lip, and he felt a secret intent there, as a familiar statue will suddenly look as if it led in its garden alcove an unauthorized life of its own.

"This is a great shock to me, naturally," she said after a while. "We've carried these responsibilities together, you and I; you have been splendid in your devotion to them, in your generosity toward people less fortunate than we are."

Her unusual praise plunged Timothy into self-abasement. "It was your generosity, Sister, not mine," he muttered. "I wouldn't have done much except for you."

Penelope ignored this confession. "I couldn't get along here without you, Timothy. There are only the two of us left since Sally passed away." Her eyes, lifted to Timothy's, filled with tears.

There had been a brother and a sister between

43

Penelope and himself; theirs and their parents' deaths had bound Timothy closely to his elder sister. He loved and admired her, and her mothering kindness to him and to Mr. Dombie, all her fine qualities, now rushed over his mind in an avenging host. Yet the more ignoble he felt the more contrary he became. He got up, walked between his accusers, and stood before the fire to bake out a kind of intestinal chill.

For Mr. Dombie was accusing him too in his silent way. Timothy looked down and saw the man's pale skull through the wisps of straw-colored hair lying loosely on it as if they had been dropped there by a casual wind that might soon blow them away again. But it's I who am monstrous, he thought.

"You are right, of course, Miss Penny," Mr. Dombie said and the words seemed to Timothy to reverberate through his past life, so often had he heard them repeated. "A sister and brother, left alone by an unhappy fate—surely you two have been drawn together by a beautiful devotion."

His husky, colorless voice robbed the words of their intended effect. The question of our devotion isn't involved, Timothy wanted to explain. But the sharp hooves galloping over his mind threw him into confusion, and he said starkly, "I think it's best for me to go away." He planted his feet a little farther apart and clasped his hands behind his back.

Penelope, her poise shattered, upset her sewing basket. By the time Timothy had crawled under the sideboard and recaptured spools, thimble, and buttons the tension in the room was broken. Penelope put the basket away behind the bunch of dried grasses on the corner table.

"We'll talk it over some other time," she said pacifically. "A good night's sleep will clear our minds about it. Are you ready for your milk punch, Mr. Dombie?"

"Yes, thank you, ma'am. We all need a good night's rest."

While Penelope went to prepare the milk punch, Timothy escorted Mr. Dombie across the hall to his bedroom. A remnant of fire drowsing in the grate had kept the room sufficiently warm. Hating his task and hating himself for it, he helped the injured man with his undressing; neither made any effort to speak, though Mr. Dombie, who had a chronic cold, hawked unpleasantly from time to time.

When Penelope knocked and handed in the milk punch, Timothy took it to Mr. Dombie and lighted the bedside candle. Before he closed the door he gave a last look about the room to see that the fire was safe and the gas turned off. Propped against the dark headboard of the walnut bed, Mr. Dombie looked white and bone-dry, like a skeleton from Timothy's student days laid out and articulated by some careful hand.

In the dining room Penelope said, "I don't think you should have broached the subject of your going away before Mr. Dombie. Naturally it would be very up-

45

setting to him." But she kissed Timothy affectionately as she left him and went up to her bedroom on the third floor.

Timothy stood by the stove and roasted himself, trying to store some heat in his bones before starting to bed. Now that the scene was ended, his suggestion of leaving home seemed unreal—when had he made this decision? In agitation he went about covering the coals with their night blanket of ashes. He blew out the lamp and scudded down the icy stairs to the floor below.

His room, being close to the ground, was like a tomb in this damp weather. The gas jet flared as he lighted it and made the chill visible. A fire was laid in the small basket grate, ready for emergencies; but this was not exactly an emergency, though his teeth chattered dismally as if in fear of a crisis getting ready to happen.

Mechanically he went to the fireplace and stood for a few minutes with his back to the lifeless grate. Penny's parting remark stirred up the creeping guilt her goodness gave him, but he still felt mean, so he fought repentance off. Instead he saw the face of the Farr girl (if that was who she was) and she seemed to give him one of her pointed, surprising smiles. It bolstered him in his meanness; his clammy extremities suddenly warmed that he had stood up to his elders and told them he wanted to go away. Would he really go? Perhaps— queerer things had happened, he silently addressed the girl, who knew what she wanted and suffered no let nor hindrance in getting it. Abruptly he took a paper spill from the vase on the mantel, lighted it at the jet, and touched it to the grate.

While the fire caught, Timothy leaned against the mantel, one leg crossed over the other, not sure in his own mind whom this negligent air was meant to impress. The kindling spluttered, the coals shifted and sank with a strange rustle of decision. The basket grate was shallow and effectual; the lightwood sent little tongues of flame through the bars, and presently the lumps of anthracite began to glow. Having a fire in his bedroom gave Timothy a novel sense of wealth and wickedness. He toasted his feet, he fiddled among his papers; he thought about his situation in the house, of his two visitors of the evening before, of his dyspepsia and of apparitions. Lying cater-cornered across his bed, he leafed through his books on magic, pretending to study up for his journey. His mind idled, making side excursions hither and yon. Happily no hypochondriacs knocked at the shop door to trouble his just repose.

Late in the night he yawned and shivered. In his self-bewitchment he had forgotten to mend the fire, which, without the magic of more coal, went out. His excursion into the deep past made him feel hoary, and he passed his hand over his black hair self-consciously. The gesture brought him back to the present, and he opened a cupboard in the bottom of the washstand and brought out a pomatum jar containing a new kind of dye. He set it on the marble top of the high bureau and leaning toward the looking glass he deftly touched his

47

side-part and the gray line beginning to show at the roots. It was his only personal vanity, this sensitiveness about his silvering hair; it seemed to stem from a vague distress because he was becoming an old man without having been a young one. The world contained so much of beauty and of ruth he never touched in his little orbit of experience.

The next morning came up clear and bitter cold. Outside the sunlight fell in powdery particles and lay drifted on the pavement. Almost immediately the shop bell began its disturbance; the sheriff's servant came for some ipecac for his master, who had eaten green fruit at night and had cholera morbus. Timothy was called on to prescribe for an old lady with heart trouble and a baby with croup. He could tell it was going to be one of those days. His young apprentice came in to help him and they pounded, weighed, mixed, and listened to symptoms without a let-up for the better part of the morning.

From time to time Timothy tried unsuccessfully to work at his desk. Papers had piled up, his fire-insurance premium had fallen due and he had a nervous itch to get it paid. There was no particular reason for this little phobia, except that the house was clapboard and he himself had come near setting it on fire once or twice while experimenting with formulae from the books of famous alchemists, whose spiritual descendant he liked to think he was. Penelope, cleaning up the debris, had

small patience with this dream and brought up quite un-
necessarily the point that as a boy he had had a bad
habit of playing with matches; so perhaps these resent-
ments, running over into the present, made him unduly
irritable when she came into the shop after a while and
said the drinking water tasted queer.

"There must be a mouse in the cistern, Timothy.
You'll have to go right away and get Ephraim to come
and clean it out."

Timothy pretended to be glued to his ledger, and indeed the page required concentration, for it was black
to the four margins with his heavy-stroked, elaborate
writing, evolved out of apothecary's dog-Latin, chemists'
symbols, and a flavor of Gothic black-letter. Penelope
came over and stood at his elbow. She said nothing; but
her stays creaked faintly with her deep breathing. This
witness to her natural urgency about everything from
mankind to mice roused Timothy's obstinacy; her vigor
chided his procrastination, so he looked up and said, "I
didn't notice any queer taste. Take some snakeroot out
of that jar, Sister, and boil it in the water if you like.
Remember how well it worked in the typhoid epidemic
last summer? Not a single case in our household, nor
among any of the customers I persuaded to boil their
drinking water with this excellent preventive—"

"I don't care," said Penelope, "it may kill germs but
it won't get the mouse out of the cistern. Mr. Dombie
and I have sensibilities, Timothy, even if you haven't.
You're so used to bad smells in here— Now make haste,
like a good fellow, and tell Ephraim to come quickly."

"Very well, Sister." Actually he had been wanting an excuse to go on a very private investigation, but out of stubbornness he kept her standing a little longer while he made a note about the insurance and meticulously counted a pile of soiled one-dollar bills from the till. Leaving the shop to the inadequate care of his apprentice, he put on his hat and coat and went out.

After the long rainy spell the sun fell on him like a rich unguent. It turned the shabby clapboards of the shop-front almost white again. In the window his big glass jars, the alchemist's sign, were kindled to potency and splendor by the lancing rays. The green and yellow reflections falling on the dusty, fly-specked jumble of cough-mixtures, corn-plasters, and nostrums lent even these a look of power. People hurried along the pavements in the sharp air, sending puffs of steam out of their nostrils like some breed of small dragons. The change in the weather infected everyone's spirits and they picked their way through the sloughs of mud with good-natured chirpings and jostlings.

Coming out of the insurance office where he had deposited his roll of bills, he followed along the Bay for a while. Behind the houses on the water side ran a frieze of masts and rigging, every rope exquisitely defined in this blue crystal air. A great heartening rumble rose from the Belgian blocks of the wide thoroughfare pounded by carts, barrows, gentlemen's carriages, drays loaded with sea-island cotton and fertilizer. In all this din Timothy, walking with his hands in the pockets of

50

his greatcoat, heard another, a tiny sound that gave him deep satisfaction: the crackling of the receipt for the insurance. He had got it paid in spite of Penelope and her contempt for the pettiness of ledgers and accounts. Well, women were like that, of course; the business of grubbing for money properly belonged to the coarser-grained sex, and Penelope's sweeping generosity was that of the non-grubber, of the spirit untarnished by contact with an account book. He was quite aware that the nods and smiles the passers-by bestowed on him were less for Dr. Partridge walking lank and solitary down the Bay than for the brother of Miss Penny—I declare, she's the most generous lady in the world—the most thoughtful—why, she'd give you the coat off her back . . .

"Yes, and the coat off mine too," said Timothy loudly, and startled a bill-collector dodging out of a doorway. "Who do you think foots the bill?"

The bill-collector gave him a wide berth and Timothy drew his head in between his shoulders like an embarrassed turtle. He was also embarrassed at being a mere grubber and at being critical of his sister's warm-heartedness. Penelope had a fling to her which he, as much as anyone, admired, whereas he didn't have much fling—at least, not in his druggist's day-by-day. It was only when he withdrew to the book-cluttered room of his fancy that he moved with largeness and style.

Reluctantly he turned a corner and walked away from East Bay. After the clatter of the Belgian blocks the quiet was like velvet, until it was broken by the

51

clippety-clop of hooves galloping in mud, and Timothy turned to see his cousin Will coming hell-for-leather down the middle of the street.

Catching sight of him, Golightly reigned in and his big roan slid to a standstill. "Howdy, Tim! What weather, eh?—after all that filthy rain. The streets are like a hog-wallow—I didn't even get out my buggy; I'd have sat all day bogged up to my middle in some cussed alley—"

"You're mud up to your middle anyhow," said Timothy.

"Well, I'm not puddling along on shanks' mare. Been to the depot yet to take your ticket for foreign parts?"

"If I was a shag-eared country doctor with nothing to do but gallop up and down the street I might go off for a while," said Timothy, standing tall and disdainful on the curb. In this waste of mud and paving stones his proposed journey seemed too illusory to mention.

"I was just going to drop off at the ice-cream parlor for a minute. Come on down and have a soda water or something."

"Still stoking the locomotive, eh?"

"Well, you got to keep your chest up," Will protested, the time-worn phrase with which he defended his adolescent's appetite, "specially when you been up half the night delivering babies first one end of town and then the other. The unreliable way women drop their young beats me—always the wrong time and the wrong place."

"Sorry I can't join you, Will. Have to do an errand and get back to the shop."

"Well, so long, then. If I was as skinny as you I'd try one of those tonics you keep in your shop-window. Why don't you take a couple of bottles of L'Elixir d'Amour?" He gave Timothy a large wink. "It might make you more soople."

Will's French accent was as rich as his English but the preposterous syllables communicated their meaning clearly to Timothy, whose French was of the same school. "So long, Will." The roan started, fell into his long stride, the satchel bounced on his croup, the mud fountained up from his flying hooves.

In spite of his stout replies, Timothy followed glumly along on the sidewalk. There was something about a man on a horse that made you feel wizened, plodding, left behind. His heart swelled up like a cabbage to be riding headlong with Will—to be tasting the magnificence of speed.

His legs, however, carried him faithfully to the tenement where Ephraim, the yard man, lived. Ephraim was out, but an old lame Negro sat against the wall of the house sunning himself and selling groundnut cakes and monkey meat from a large flat basket. A group of colored children drawn by the rich smell of the molasses clustered around, jigging, shrieking, and tormenting him. Timothy bought a few moment's quiet by taking ten cents' worth of the chewy candy and distributing it. The old man gladly contracted to send Ephraim a mes-

53

sage to go to Miss Penny Partridge's right away. Having full faith in the efficacy of the grapevine Timothy let the matter rest there, but before leaving he asked him if Mr. Charley Farr didn't live somewhere in that part of town.

With extreme deliberation the Negro drew closer about him the soiled scarlet coat he wore, a survival of some long-discarded style. It had the look of a theatrical property or even of a disguise—at least a suggestion that under the appearances of everyday lay something more. The old fellow consulted the children with quick glances and cryptic monosyllables that excluded a white man, left him isolated in the midst of a conspiracy even the babies seemed to be part of. Finally they vouchsafed directions of a sort for finding the house, directions that might equally answer for the pursuit of wild antelopes.

The attempt meant going a long way round. Timothy sent a defiant look in the direction of the shop, rammed his hands in his pockets, and walked rapidly toward the section where the Farrs lived. His problem was not insoluble, however; he found a corner grocer with a prosaic mind who identified the house for him. He approached it, strolling now with an air of nonchalance, and examined it from across the street. It was a noncommittal dwelling, its shutters bowed in against the sun and other intruders. His dark-browed vixen was nowhere to be seen. Not a flowerpot gave a clew to the inhabitants; he craned hopefully at the clothesline in the back yard, but it was bare of informative evidence. Presently a pretty, plump girl came along and went through the back gate with a basket on her arm, having evidently been to market. It seemed unlikely that she was at all related to anyone capable of seething the fat of infants in a copper cauldron.

Timothy started home feeling quite irritable. What a wild goose chase on a busy morning—and only that hydrocephalous boy left to mind the shop. A horse-car took him part of the way, but the chivalry of the driver necessitated so many unscheduled stops to put ladies out at their own front doors that he could have walked the distance in less time. When he went into the hall to hang his hat and coat on the hatrack, he saw through the open door of his room that Penny was there laying a fresh fire. Bracing himself, he went in and forestalled the expected accusation of self-indulgence. "It was so damp and cold last night, Sister; I really needed a blaze. There's lots of grippe going round, you know—"

Penelope stood up with the coal scuttle in her hand and looked at him with large blue eyes. "Why, of course, Timothy; it was bitter last night. Of course you needed a fire. You must never endanger your health—and besides, a little fire is such a pleasure and comfort, isn't it? There's nothing I love more than falling asleep with the firelight on the ceiling. But how muddy you are! Take off those damp clothes quickly and let me put them in the kitchen to dry." She went outside to allow him privacy and Timothy handed his clothes to her through the door, feeling doubly guilty to have so misjudged his sister. Far from being censorious . . . All during their midday dinner he made amends (knowing this was the way to please her) by asking Mr. Dombie about the battle at Secessionville and simulating a great interest in the oft-told tale. The high tragedy of that small engagement crumbled among the dry husks of Mr. Dombie's speech. For him, too, it was an oft-told tale; the immediacy had leached away; his sacrifice had gone to join the faded heroisms of other old battles. He stalked among the gleanings, pecking at details . . . "our line ran north and south . . . only eighty men in the rifle-pits . . . we held the pits four hours and twenty minutes." Or he would tell a little joke, his thin neck shooting forward. "I was reported dead, you know. Officially I'm a corpse—ha-ha. Miss Penny, ma'am, how do you like having a corpse at table?"

Shuddering slightly, Penny said—as usual: "Hush, you mustn't say such things, Mr. Dombie."

No one mentioned Timothy's ill-considered idea of going away.

After dinner Mr. Dombie took a siesta, following which he usually came and sat for an hour or so by the stove in the shop and made paper spills from old news-papers. This saving on matches was his chief contribu-tion to the economy of the household and he made a great many spills; every empty jar and mantel-vase bristled with them. Presently Penelope came through the shop dressed for the street. The cold weather brought a rosy-violet color into her cheeks, and in spite of her rusty black she looked warm and vital, a woman in the full tide of life carrying under the maternal flow of her cloak great gifts of energy and reassurance.

"Here's a letter for you, Mr. Dombie. It came by the afternoon mail." Handing him the envelope, she paused by the stove for a moment. "No bad news, I hope."

Mr. Dombie turned it in his hand and opened it deliberately. There was silence in the shop as he looked over the contents. He returned it to the envelope and said aloofly, "No, no—merely a business communication." He put it into his pocket.

Penelope stood by, silent; three vertical lines marred her fine forehead. Her patience with Mr. Dombie was infinite, but his secretiveness about the rare letters that came to the house for him irked her incontinently. Delicacy forbade her questioning him too closely about his relatives, since they seemed to have abandoned or forgotten him; he so seldom mentioned his past, his life before the War, that he too might have forgotten, or have had none. The envelopes usually bore the imprint of the bank in which he kept what small funds he possessed. It was downright obstinate of him, Penelope sometimes grumbled to Timothy, considering they gave him food, lodging, and medicines, not to take them into his confidence about his affairs.

But Mr. Dombie went back to making spills, and she had to go out with her curiosity unassuaged. Timothy had his own irritations; every time the door opened Mr. Dombie greeted the newcomer with a monsoon of a sneeze. He cross-questioned each customer about his errand: "How's that—sore throat? It may be diph-theria. Have you observed a membrane like a white patch in the throat?" Or, "So Mrs. Button has had a stroke. I've been expecting it for some time. Her left side is completely paralyzed? A poultice of corn meal—"

Many of his customers, Timothy knew, were put off by this morbid interest in people's illnesses. He glanced at the withered figure in the rocking chair, kept for him near the stove. Still, Mr. Dombie was a responsibility they had to carry, the stranger within their gates, the man who had been brought to this pitiful wreckage by a holy war in his and Penelope's defense. Once in a while Timothy wondered what Mr. Dombie would have been like had his bones and his nervous system not been damaged by a Union shell, but whatever the answer was, he had to admit that holy wars can do fearful things to decent people. He couldn't help noting, however, that he made no further sales that afternoon except a five-cent package of Epsom salts.

Timothy took advantage of this lull to work on his ledgers. His mind tugged to be free to consider the enigmas of the past three days; but privacy was hard to come by in his routine, so he glumly balanced his petty cash account. Actually, the shop hadn't done so badly. If Sister would just restrain her incontinent goodness— It came into his head that he might take a leaf from Mr. Dombie's bankbook and have an account of his own without divulging it to Penelope. He let out a small mischievous chuckle at the thought. He could put a per-centage of his earnings into it every month, and in time he would have enough to take a trip. He would harden his heart to Penelope's just demands. Of course he would always take care of her; just how he would manage it if he went away was a detail that would have to be worked out.

By evening the weather had softened; the cistern was purged of the mouse and other inadvertent guests, but it was bedtime before Timothy escaped the entanglements of domesticity and found a moment to be alone. He went into the shop, and when he had barred the door he turned to the shelf where the Epsom salts concealed the pot of ointment, forgotten until his last sale of the afternoon had exposed it in its corner. He took off the lid and looked at the dark, oleaginous salve with a speculative eye; the smell of it filled his head and produced a queer exhilaration; he started to scoop it out, then hesitated, feeling mildly foolish with the dry mood of his day of buying and selling still crusted on him like salt crystals. He, a respectable pharmacist, giving credence to strange powers in this small crock in his hand; he, a member of the Reverend Batt's congregation, going over, or rather gone over, to the dimension of sorcery—for on the instant all doubts were sponged away that uncommon results would follow his dipping a finger into this mixture.

He must make up his mind quickly, he thought, because a sort of momentum was gathering him up and fear, the good witch who warns against danger, lost substance moment by moment. But the mind, he went further, isn't framed for this kind of question . . . there

are times to recognize its limitations . . . a sudden revulsion shook him against all that was tight and classical,
against the literal eye and the aggregate of facts like
crushed rock.

He scooped out the ointment and rubbed it energetically on the backs of his hands.

Immediately they began to burn and he walked about
shaking them gently while he waited, full of curiosity
and childish hope, to see what would happen. The burning increased, he fanned the air more vigorously; then
faint laughter rolled on the waves of stirred air and a
faraway voice cried something like "Ride out!" He
looked wildly around the empty shop; the muffled cries
went on, like words corked in a bottle. He thought faint
squeaks were coming from the twinkling jars about him
and ran dizzily from one shelf to another like a large
bird that had flown down the chimney and flapped about
to escape. But now the sounds came from outside—he
sprang into the nearest shop window, scattering the medicines on display, and pressed against the pane. The cold
cloudy air beyond rustled with motion, with figures
(though he couldn't make them out at all clearly) rising
and spinning round the high white porch of the church
steeple and coasting breakneck down a long beam of
darkness to the soft earth. A bass viol was playing such
a gay minor tune as his ears had never heard—it seemed
to be a salamander, from its sharp bow-arm, that was
dispensing this gipsy music. Timothy struggled to get
through the transparence that shut him in from a world
so irresponsible, so light-footed and menacing. Let me

out—let me out, he muttered, running his hands over the invisible wall of his jail. He reached up, standing on tiptoe, toward the dancers, he almost rose from the platform; then suddenly his excitement dropped from under him, he had to catch himself to keep from falling. The burning of his hands slacked off, the dizziness passed, leaving a heavy languor in all his limbs. Cautiously skirting the green carboy, he let himself down to the floor of the shop like a man escaped from jeopardy, breathing heavily at this sharp change to another element.

Little by little the stove, the counter, the cases, slipped into focus; glass and iron and wood crowded round him. He went over to the sink and scrubbed his hands with a detergent; then turning out the gas he stumbled across the hall to bed.

The next day was Sunday. The Partridge household going to church remarked on the first beady buds strung along the branches. They walked slowly because of Mr. Dombie, who swung each foot forward stiffly and at random as if it didn't belong to him, but luckily their church was just down the block, an easy distance for a pair of crutches.

At the church door other members of the congregation gathered round them, soothing and sibilant. On Sunday came Penelope's harvest of reward for her many kindnesses; and Timothy shared in the love and praise that curled about them like incense as they went up the aisle. Not that they would have deemed incense appro-

61

priate to this service, but their expressions indicated that some kind of sweet smoke gratified their Low-Church nostrils. Timothy had retained only a vague recollection of his experience of the evening before and, strangely, he thought very little about it. What remained chiefly was a complacent acceptance of a state of affairs he had suspected all along, namely, that the rationalists were of all superstitious people the best-deluded. Besides, he did not consider the Lord's Day suitable for admitting such speculations, having grave doubts under whose dominion the world he had discovered lay. To most of this congregation the Devil was quite real, always at one's elbow, he could even be at church on Sundays, not a pewholder exactly but an interested attendant. Until he could work things out, Timothy had no desire to attract the attention of either a chastening God or the Author of Lies.

During the collection he glanced idly about. The proximity of a pretty young girl in a pew on the side fluttered him pleasurably. He looked at her across the wooden partition as at a green pasture beyond a fence. He knew her, indeed he had once thought he might marry her—as soon as I see my way clear— But things kept happening to prevent and she remained to this day in ignorance of his private intention. . . . The scene before him altered a little, two figures stood near the pulpit, the asthmatic singsong of the organ dropped to a murmur, the vox humana became his own voice, manly, confident, taking the charming Sylvia for his wife. The vox angelica responded gladly, a trilling acceptance. . . . The daydream, as always, had power to dissolve such facts as the pew beneath him, the solid persons of Penelope and Mr. Dombie beside him, which persons it was his plain duty to nourish and support. He continued blissfully to conjure up the wedding and the transports that might be expected to follow soon after, remaining bolt upright like a bashaw when the final blessing rocked the rows of worshippers forward in unison.

On Sundays the shop was closed but Timothy always stayed at home during the afternoon in case of emergency calls. He drowsed and read in one of the armchairs by the dining-room fire, and to him this was the high point of the week, although Mr. Dombie sat there too and shared even this time of indulgence. Penelope went visiting.

Luckily no tinklings from below spoiled the beautiful peace of the Sabbath, and the hour for their evening tea passed without notice. It was only when Penelope rushed in, calling to him up the stairs, that Timothy realized she had, remarkably for her, come home late. He jumped up and opened the dining-room door. She appeared out of the darkness of the hall roseate and panting.

"I've just been to see Lena Whitlock, Timothy, and found she had a collapse this morning. I've got a nurse, but she can't come on until later, so I'm going back to stay until she arrives."

"How dreadful!" Timothy murmured, seeing Lena Whitlock, a kind, brown little woman who sewed out, as he had sometimes seen her in this house helping

Penelope make over her dresses. "Poor soul—is she in a bad way?"

"Dr. Porter has been working over her and thinks he has pulled her through this attack. But he says it's only a question of time."

"Very sad—very sad," said Mr. Dombie. "What ails the poor lady?"

"Some obscure disease, apparently; hard to diagnose. But I say it's too early to give up hope. If only she could take a sea voyage—the change of air might work a miracle—"

"What are her symptoms?" Mr. Dombie wanted to know. "Has she a fever? Vomiting? Cancer, now, is an obscure disease—fools the doctors—"

But Penny for once was in no mood to oblige Mr. Dombie. She shrugged off his helpful diagnosis and went about putting the tea cloth on the table. Her long black cloak stirred the plush-curtained air of the room as she moved; her momentum had a sureness about it from an emotion competently controlled. She looked almost beautiful.

"I have two prescriptions, dear—can you fill them? I must get back directly."

Timothy gladly went down to the shop for the sake of Lena Whitlock, bent over a sewing machine or kneeling on the floor with her mouth full of pins. A widow too, with three little girls to support. Luckily he was able to supply the medicine; he labeled the bottles and took them to Penelope as she came down into the lower hall.

"I'll escort you back, Sister. It's too late for you to be going through the streets alone."

"I don't mind in the slightest. You stay here, dear, and give Mr. Dombie his supper."

Penelope was never afraid for herself; still, she shouldn't go about alone after dark. As he stood torn between conflicting duties, she smilingly took the bottles from him and went out with them.

Timothy put some cold victuals on a tray and fed Mr. Dombie and himself. Mr. Dombie for once felt talkative. He paid a fine tribute to Penelope's good heart and good sense, and then began to question Timothy about the treatment of convulsions in children. A niece of his had nearly died with a convulsion; while she had recovered, it had left her in delicate health. Weary of the limited range of Mr. Dombie's conversation, Timothy sank deeper into his high collar and his book. Taking a low advantage of Penny's absence, he even answered, "Pshaw!" or "Fiddlesticks!" once or twice.

When he had helped Mr. Dombie to bed, Timothy banked the fire and went to fetch Penelope home. Lena lived across town, but he was used to walking, and stepped out briskly—though a fog was coming in, and the trees turned to vapor, the seaward streets choked into silence, made him fidgety. As he approached Lena's gate Dr. Porter had just lifted the iron weight tethering his horse and was putting it into the buggy.

"Good evening, Doctor; and how is Miss Lena this evening?"

65

"Ah—" The doctor's deprecatory sigh floated down the mist, dissolved and left a vacuum, the signature of death. "It seems to be leucocythemia, but the symptoms are irregular. In any case I fear there's little hope."

The nurse had arrived, so at Timothy's ring Penelope put on her cloak and came with him. The fog had worked selectively to blot out familiar landmarks, leaving parts that were subtly estranged by their separation from the whole. Front steps led menacingly up to vanished doors; iron fences, their scrollings suddenly sharp and black, barred the passer-by from the unhallowed country beyond, whose mother-of-pearl air was surely breathed by a race of different beings. Crossing a little park they came abruptly on a church, a long white flank and steeple, couched in the mist. "Why, it looks like a unicorn!" said Timothy.

He could have believed it *was* a unicorn, but Penelope could not, so she answered with an irritated "Tsch-tsch!" It was plain that, coming from Lena's sickroom, she was not in an imaginative mood, which he thought a pity, considering that she possessed the traditional requirements for catching and taming such a quarry. But one couldn't allude to one's sister's virginity, crowning virtue though it was, so he contented himself with saying regretfully, "It would make an unusual pet."

"You're absurdly credulous, Timothy; I wish you'd outgrow it."

"Of course I'm credulous. I can believe anything." He stalked beside her boastfully, more vertical than ever

66

in his long black coat, now rimed with tiny gray drops. "There are unicorns in the Bible," he added.

"Don't be trivial. It passes my understanding how you can accept science and religion and still have so many silly superstitions. It's so inconsistent."

"But in this world you have to be inconsistent to have any faith at all. The scientists don't know much when you come right down to it; simple people often make fools of them, they get there first by a short cut—by intuition, if you like. Besides, it seems to me you are the inconsistent one; how can you believe the Bible, the Word of God, and not accept its witness that witches and familiar spirits work through the world?"

"With God nothing is impossible, of course," said Penelope tranquilly, "but it is not for us to meddle in such dangerous matters." In the deathly, muffled streets this sentiment sounded particularly apt, so Timothy dropped the argument. They crossed the street to the church, and, as they turned and walked beside it, he dragged his forefinger along the white sweating plaster and was not surprised to discover that the timorous beast had escaped his coarse male touch by becoming a church again.

In spite of her fatiguing day Penelope walked buoyantly, indeed the asperity of the night air seemed to exhilarate her. She went back to the subject of Lena Whitlock. "I don't believe she's beyond hope," she said with combat in her voice. "Dr. Porter gives up too easily, I'm afraid."

67

"He knows his business, Sister. You always say yourself that he's a splendid diagnostician—much better than Will."

Penelope made her doctor, her minister, her greengrocer, subjects of ardent partisanship, so this answer fetched her up short. She merely repeated, "He gives up too soon—I wouldn't be beaten so easily." Timothy felt in his nerve-ends that she was leading somewhere, a road he might balk at taking, so again he let the conversation drop and they walked the rest of the way in silence.

When they came into the entry hall Penelope thanked her brother warmly for bringing her home. "You'd better catch up the fire to go to bed by, Timothy. Your clothes are damp and you mustn't get a chill." She followed him into his bedroom and put a match to the grate herself.

Timothy, easily touched by her solicitude, mumbled his thanks self-consciously. There was a look of the wise woman about Penelope stooping by the hearth, her long dark garments piled about her, and stirring the fire which sprang to life under her hands and shed a broken light on her strong, intent face. She looked up over her shoulder. "Timothy, I think we should send Lena on a sea voyage." Timothy was silent. "I hate to ask you for more money, but I spent all my surplus refitting that Murphy family after they were burnt out. Lena is a fine woman; the little money I've paid her is no compensation for the faithful service she has given us."

68

"But, Sister, it's no use—you heard what Dr. Porter said." He made a rough mental calculation of the journey's cost.

"You can only try."

Timothy walked over to the bookcase and leaned against it as if the magic it contained might stiffen his backbone. He ran his hands into his trouser pockets.

"Sister, I know you'll think I'm selfish, but you'll have to find the money somewhere else. I've decided to start saving to go to England."

Penelope flowed up to her full height with a rippling of heavy cloth. "England!" She seemed consciously to turn the weight of tallness and darkness on her shorter brother. "I can't go about begging, Timothy. Besides, we should be the ones to do this. It's never yet been said of us that we failed in our responsibilities. I'm willing to save every cent—I'll contribute all I can to the expenses."

"There are other people who can afford it better than we can."

"You can't be serious about going off and leaving the shop, the house—us? What, may I ask, would become of Mr. Dombie and me? We couldn't live here alone."

The fire sent out a ribald tongue between the iron lips of the grate and made a small glare in Timothy's brain. "Mr. Dombie could go away," he said and he felt his mouth draw up at the corners, against his will, into a wicked smile. "He speaks of having a niece—he could go to live with her. This house is too expensive for us, anyway. We could sell it and you could live with Cousin

69

Lou Partridge for a while. You always say you love her dearly."

"I do indeed—it would be a joy and a privilege to live with Cousin Lou. But we know nothing of Mr. Dombie's niece. She must be an unnatural relative never to have written nor come to see him in all this time. Would you turn him out of the house, Timothy? The Devil must have gotten into you to make you think of such a thing!"

Well, let him stand by me then, thought Timothy. Aloud he said, "We've done our part by Mr. Dombie, Sister. For twenty years we've housed and fed him and never said what we both know—that he's sponged on us. He's never made any attempt to go back to his kin. You say they've never come to see him—has he ever tried to find them? Maybe they think he's dead. The truth is that he'd rather stay here and let us support him—"

The Devil must really possess him, Timothy thought. He had never phrased these horrors before, even in his mind.

"Speak for yourself," said Penelope, and her words took on an unintended significance. "It has been my happiness and satisfaction to take care of Mr. Dombie— a victim of war, needing my strength—" She began to walk stormily up and down the cluttered room, scattering the piles of papers with the flounce of her skirt.

"That's because he agrees with everything you say!" cried Timothy, finding that this as much as anything was his grudge against Mr. Dombie.

Penelope turned and threw him a look like a sharp

stone. The quarrel was having a peculiar effect on her. The more she took the part of the good, the generous, the unselfish, the less it seemed to become her. Her grave beauty of the earlier evening had gone without a trace. Her eyes were distraught; the smooth surface of her face had puckered into little planes of dark and light, which did not conceal her bitter wilfulness.

She said, "You did not go through what I did to save Mr. Dombie. That night in the hospital . . . I had to search for him among the dead . . . it was almost as if I went down into the grave to bring him back. I will not give him up."

A quality in Penelope's voice more than the actual words tingled unpleasantly along Timothy's nerves, a morbidity he had never recognized in her before. They stood together unmasked in the room after all these years and their nakedness was indecent and dreadful.

Penelope heaved a great sigh and came back to herself. The revelation clouded, hung on the hairline that divides the horrible from the ridiculous and fell back into absurdity. She said with quite ordinary sisterly badgering, "You've always had a commercial streak in you, Timothy, but I never knew what base materialism you were capable of."

This was a telling shot; Timothy's own knowledge of himself convicted him. He became aware that he was clutching the leather purse in his pocket and remained silent.

Penelope went on. "And now you are going to let

71

that poor woman die and her children depend on charity so you can travel, forsooth, and visit the Crystal Palace!"

Timothy saw the dome split wide and send its bright splinters right and left. Penelope's demand was logic-proof—the poor widow, the orphan children. He hated her for being right as he had never hated in his life before.

"Very well, Sister; Lena shall go, but this is the last time you'll get money from me."

Penelope's sudden triumph unnerved her. She clawed at the collar of her dress, stretching her neck this way and that. Then she went silently toward the door, stumbling a little over the rumpled pamphlets. "May God forgive us," she said without turning. "I will go and pray. I beg you to do the same."

But Timothy watched her in despair as she crossed the threshold because he knew his final threat to her was vain.

Timothy sat down and gazed at the door that Penelope had from ineradicable habit closed behind her. He could hear her going softly up the stairs to her chilly bedroom two floors above his own. Then he stood up again, put his head back, and looked for a long time at the ceiling; and having in his heightened state some power to see through lath and plaster, he perceived Mr. Dombie recumbent over his head and Penny above them both. Slowly the ceiling began to come down on

72

him in a barely perceptible descent; he blinked hard and saw instead his herb compress and the sticky juices that trickled from the leaves and stalks as it squeezed them.

Presently his pale serious face returned to the perpendicular and he stood for a moment twisting one hand with the other as if compelled to wreak himself an injury. Then he went over and leaned on the marble top of the bureau. The looking glass gave back the same muffled and melancholy countenance he was used to and the same high, narrow shoulders. Yet he was teased by a likeness he could not name; it was as if a draftsman, without changing a feature, had brought out certain traits by a deft touch here and there of the charcoal. The mustache he wore as a refuge and a disguise seemed no longer to hide the slight lift of his lips at the corners; his lank black hair looked like a foreigner's. His flesh pimpled over with the chill of exposure and strangeness.

Dreadful as the unmasking of Penelope had been, he feared worse this half-lit presence within himself. Yet— if he accepted its dominion, would it break that other, that lifelong dominion over him? In a spurt of action he lighted the lamp on his night table; as the flame rose from the wick it made a yellow circle on the ceiling and dissolved the gray shadows. He ran over to the fireplace and piled on fresh coal until the little black nuggets fell off and rolled among the papers on the carpet. The grate responded to his excitement with a furious crackling.

73

Well, what can you do in a situation like this? I'm damned if I do and damned if I don't, he said, with a great full sigh.

He turned to his books, his handy substitute for moral decision. He opened a bookcase, and from long-established habit took out a volume at random and opened it, looking for a sign, a message, an instruction from some unformulated power. *Travels in Arabia, American Female Poets Illustrated*—he threw them on the floor and went on to the next bookcase.

The top shelves, neglected and forbidding, bent their carved walnut frown upon him; he brought a chair and stood on it, pulling down the sagging, dusty volumes. But the invertebrate back numbers of *Littell's Living Age, Sermons on Sundry Occasions*—these offered him no magical formulae. Delphi remained silent.

The Farr girl, he thought, treading restlessly up and down, because he had taken off his shoes and the cane-bottomed chair cut through his soles, would burst into raucous laughter if she could see him now. She, he felt sure, would be able to decide confidently between two evils; she would not have given up a resolve through cowardice. For it was not Penelope's fault, he owned justly. As the eldest she had properly taken over the family and managed its affairs after their parents' death, and he had let her. It was his habit of defeatism, the too-willing acceptance, that had brought him to this moment. The Farr girl, he thought, wishing he had a name to call her by, knew what she wanted and took it —even a jar of frogs—for of course she had taken them, for some obscure reason, or for no reason except that she wanted them.

The room became bright and furiously hot. His palms and his forehead sweated gently. He got off the chair and sat down on it, feeling Penelope stand over him, bending on him, like the bookcases, a carven frown. Suddenly he said with rancor, Why, she's half a head taller than me! No woman, he thought, ever used half a head to such advantage.

He thought of an old prop and mainstay in times of dread and wondered why he had not tried it before. He padded over to his bedside table and picked up the Bible—the new Bible Penny had given him for his birthday. But a great reluctance to open it seized him; he went back to the fire and looked into the blazing coals for some time. Then he resolutely inserted his thumbnail between the thin pages and parted them.

The fine print spun before his eyes, reversed, settled itself in ordered lines, just above his finger-tip.

"I know where thou dwellest, even where Satan's throne is—"

The fire crackled and spat, and he turned his back to cool his scorched face. Then he twirled to the light and reread the passage.

So, Sister had been right again. And by being right, had once more put him in the wrong. Permanently, it now appeared.

In an abandonment of rage against her he tried to tear the Bible in half, but its stout new covers balked his pulling and jerking. He threw it on top of the coals;

75

a gasp came from the grate as the supple leaves ignited. He went over to the wardrobe, took out his coat and hat. The stench of burning leather closed his nostrils and his throat, the red light of the upward flames leapt on the wall as he jerked the door open and went out coughing into the street.

The cold and dampness touched Timothy's senses with healing as he tramped along between the sleeping houses. The fog had shredded and was moving inland, leaving a spectral shine on railings and window-ledges, like the tracks of an army of snails. In his urge to get away he merely followed the street for several blocks until he could go no farther. What stopped him at last was an iron railing, and beyond it the river in which misty stars swam. He walked about between the hushed trees, surprised only that he felt no fear of the darkness and the emptiness of the park in which he found himself. If the supernatural beings to whom he had given a back-door allegiance couched in the grottoes of shadow behind him, he was now indifferent to their spells and their mischief.

He had no inkling of the hour except that a late moon leaned a sunken cheek on the eastern bar of the harbor. His feet hurt because he had forgotten his shoes in his dash from the house, but he was indifferent to them also. He turned westward beside the quiet river and at length left it behind him, following soundlessly an irregular course along incurious streets. Questions floated through his mind, light and random as milkweed floss. What did it mean to belong to the Devil? His poor dead mother would feel badly for him about this. Yet he felt uncertain about it all. The throne of Satan—it rang in his head with a sonority he couldn't but admire; damnation had a high style, at least. . . .

He came out by a large pond set like a pane of glass in the leaden earth. A faint reddening had begun in the sky behind him but he held on to the night, to the west reflected at his feet; the mysterious image of the firmament, the tall and punctual constellations keeping their rendezvous in this still place—as his thoughts ran thus, a small star broke loose from the patterned sky and plunged in a bright arc toward the swallowing horizon. How art thou fallen from Heaven, O Lucifer, son of the morning! Perhaps lesser devils are being born all the time. Perhaps one is born tonight.

His inner fires burned lower; in spite of his thick socks his feet were icy on the flagstones and he turned eastward toward home. He felt inhuman skimming along with no footfalls in this steep corridor walled with brick and wood. The glow in the east had brightened and sounds crept down the street toward him of people awake and stirring; a far metallic clanking streaked the quietude. The glow, he discovered, was not in its proper place, it was a little north of east, it came from a fire, not the sun. But the boyish impulse to run to a fire did not throb strongly enough and he kept his direction at the same pace. When he reached the center of the town he began to encounter people running, lumpy figures also unreal, yet with a different unreality from his own.

77

The street he followed cut across his own at right angles. He reached the corner and turned into a lane of fiery color that smeared the sky and even the mud puddles in the street itself. Crowds of people, black and grotesque in their thick clothes, stood in a semicircle; the sight of the steepled flames licking around his own roof somehow caused him no surprise. He approached the silhouetted backs, unable to check his momentum.

As he reached the barrier made by the crowd a woman turned and looked at him. "Dr. Partridge!" Her scream tore a rent in the line of backs; as if he had been an apparition people fell away on either side and his name ricocheted along the street from mouth to mouth. Their shrinking stopped him in his tracks; he took it for accusation until Will Golightly ran up, looking demonic himself with his shirt torn and soot all over his face, and seized him by the arm.

"Timothy! We thought you— For God's sake, how did you escape?"

A new kind of cunning prompted Timothy's reply. "I went out—'way across town—on a sick call."

Will threw his arms about him and almost suffocated him with a great muscular anguish. "Poor fellow—poor fellow! We did everything we could to save them— before God, we did!" Timothy felt his blood thick in his veins; his ears were as sluggish as his tongue and only fragments of information came through to him . . . fire must have started on the ground floor . . . stairway a roaring furnace . . . they were cut off on the second floor . . . the hook and ladder mired in Church Street . . .

78

So, the dark forces that rule our lives, whether of pre-
destination or of anarchy, had taken a hand in this
event. The miring of the hook and ladder was quite
outside the scope of his imagination or his carelessness.
People began to crowd around and pour their pity over
him like oil on his burns; and indeed the great heat of
the fire was beginning to scorch his hands and face. The
roaring of the fanged flames as they consumed the clapboards, the slow tilt and crash of the cornice and part of
the roof, forbade either hope or fear that anyone within
might still live. The firemen had given up a fruitless task
and were lymphatically pouring water on the adjoining
houses.

Utter confusion lay over the street before the gutted
shop. The wooden mortar and pestle that had hung
above the door rolled about among a jumble of bottles,
jugs, and instruments. The boots of the firemen ground
his glass carboys under, the gaudy liquids dark on the
pavement. Little had been saved, and that at random—
someone had lugged out the bellows from the shop, as
if the fire might languish.

Now only the supports of the house stood, looming
like charred ribs against the roaring gold and vermilion
behind them. As Timothy watched, he became conscious of a prickling at the back of his neck, and a moni-
tor within warned him that someone was staring at him.
Behind him in the raw light he saw his visitor of a few
days ago. Only her face was visible across the high intervening shoulders, but he distinctly made out her eloquent eyes fixed on him. He could not translate their

79

gaze, secretive, yet full of communications. For what seemed a long time they looked at each other in a sort of partnership, separated from the rest of the crowd. Then she pushed aside the man in front of her, slipped through the opening, and went away along the edge of the circle of watchers, carrying some kind of bundle under her long shawl.

Timothy seized Will's arm. "Who's that, Will—that girl over there near the fire horses?" But Will did not understand him, or perhaps did not understand such a question at such a time. He put his arm around Timothy and said, "No good staying here any longer, Tim; there's nothing we can do, nothing anyone can do now. We must leave their souls to God. Come on home and get to bed. You'll just catch rheumatism out in this cold."

Timothy had no will either to go or to stay, so he let Golightly pilot him through the crowd. The staring eyes, full of horror and pity, peppered his face as if with a burning rash. It was a relief when the coolness and darkness of the next street closed round him. Golightly drew him along to his own house, where a light burned and where his wife greeted them with puffing solicitude but spared him the necessity for comment. She prepared a bed and some hot food and left him alone in her company room.

The sky was bright now with the true dawn. Timothy wrapped himself in Will's voluminous nightshirt and, climbing into the high bed, slept all day without waking.

80

Part Two

IN THE time following the fire the sense of unreality continued and grew stronger in Timothy, only sometimes it was he who seemed unreal and sometimes it was the world of appearances. Will and Anna Maria were kindness itself and urged him to live with them in their large drafty house. But their sympathy caused him acute dismay. He managed by some happy trick of the mind not to think of the horror which had befallen Penelope and Mr. Dombie; he continued to picture them as they had been in life. He could not imagine Penelope in particular as destructible by any earthly means, indeed the thought sometimes crossed his mind that she might still be about, having escaped the fire in some such way as he himself had. But if she walked the earth she did not appear in any of her accustomed places, and as his shocked nerves stirred and quivered back to normal this morbid notion faded away.

For a while business and legal matters engaged him

deeply, since the inheritance of money has a way of dis-
lodging non-material preoccupations, even curiosity and
fear. Penelope had named him the sole heir of her
estate, which consisted of a small competence in bonds
and her share of the house, now represented by the fire
insurance, happily paid up. But the airing of Mr.
Dombie's affairs brought two sharp surprises. First,
Mr. Dombie was discovered to have had a substantial
sum of money tucked away in his bank box and savings
account. A spurt of sympathy tempered the annoyance
Timothy felt at this unfairness to him; their lodger had
stood off Penelope's inquisitiveness to that extent at
least. Did he too have some secret hope, some scheme of
getting away? The second surprise came at him head on
out of Mr. Dombie's brief will. This money was left, not
to Penelope as might have been expected, but to him.
How vexed Sister would have been! He forgave Mr.
Dombie the repetitious monologues, the loud self-pity-
ing sneezes, the apathy toward everybody, including
Timothy, his host.

His indifference to his kin, if he had any, was matched
by their indifference to him. The War seemed to have
made a clean end to his life before that time. Perhaps
they had received the official report of his death; at any
rate, no one appeared to dispute Timothy's inheritance.

Will was greatly excited about Timothy's sudden
accession to what was, relatively, riches. He returned
to his argument that Timothy should go away. "You
need a change, man—a new outlook. It's an ill wind

that blows nobody any good. You ought to travel for a while, see London and Paris—then take a turn with some of the big drug companies in New York."

Timothy was glad Will knew nothing of his conversion to the idea of traveling nor of the arguments it had bred in his household. It rescued him from the dilemma of explaining what he scarcely understood himself, namely, that his desire to go away seemed to have been cauterized by the fire. He took long walks about the streets by day and by night and found among them a compulsion to stay, a sense of a design yet unfinished.

People tactfully left him alone, though they stared at him over their shoulders as he passed. He concluded without vanity that his appearance must be singular, especially when a gray swath began to make its appearance along the part in his black thatch. He took to the side streets and alley-ways to avoid curious eyes, looking at houses and gardens with fresh pleasure as the spring began to stir in the winter branches.

As he was coming home one evening along a street near the waterfront his eye fell on a house set far back at the end of a narrow lot. It was a stuccoed house, its yellowish face mottled by wind and rain; and as he looked at it in the falling dusk he felt a shock like recognition, though he had no clear recollection of having noticed it before. He stood with his hands on the little iron gate that led in from the street and looked along the strip of weedy ground that ran like a length of drugget to the front steps. He couldn't tell whether it was occupied or not, but he guessed not from an air of reserved expectancy with which its windows looked out from under the shaggy trees around it.

He left it reluctantly and walked past the next building, a livery stable, lingering a little there to enjoy the smell of musty grain and leather, and the bustling sounds of men and horses. Now with his new wealth, he would get a horse perhaps—

The next day he strolled by and looked at the house again, thinking that the illusion of dusk might have endowed it with false significance. The daylight did indeed reveal an unpromising mansion, narrow, withdrawn, and obviously untenanted except for a brindled cat that walked along the high wall and looked at him with pale hostile eyes. But again he had the quiver of recognition, of subcutaneous assent—and he felt sure that the dormers under their hoods of dark red tiles would have a pretty view of the harbor.

His conjectures about the house proved astonishingly correct; it had been empty for some years because the owners refused to put improvements on it and because of the undesirable proximity of the stable. Improvements did not bulk large among the luxuries Timothy intended to indulge in, and he liked the smell of livery stables; furthermore, the third-floor front did look out on a blue and bewitching section of water between other roofs, all the more provocative to him because of being framed, enclosed, limited—like a small private sea. He was able to buy the house for cash at a very moderate price.

Negotiating the deal gave him great satisfaction, and when the moment came to pay, the sight of his name on a check of such size filled him with awe and admiration. He walked back to the Golightlys' in a state of excitement he had not felt since the fire. He found Will sitting by the parlor hearth with all the windows open.

"Come in, Tim! God bless me, where have you been? You don't find it chilly in here, do you? It's a fine evening; you ought to be out riding through the pine woods. Thank your stars you didn't go in for medicine. Why I chose to spend my life tied down by a lot of croupy babies and puking adults is beyond me. A man hasn't got but one life to live—"

"You'll have to stay at home and tend to your family and your guest if you let in the night air like this," said his wife, coming in and putting down the windows. Anna Maria always panted a little as if her fine deep bosom were too heavy a load for the mere breath of life to lift. "Well, Timothy, what have you been doing with yourself?" She joined them at the fire, pushing her way as best she could among the dogs stretched out on the rug.

"That's what I'd like to know." Will looked along his nose at Timothy with sharp curiosity, the gray bristles thrusting pugnaciously from his nostrils. "You're on the prowl all day, doing nothing that I can see."

"I bought a house this afternoon," said Timothy tranquilly. "I shall be leaving you before long, as soon as I can get it cleaned up a bit."

"A house!" cried the Golightlys together, astounded

87

and a little affronted, he could see, that he had not consulted them, nor even hinted at his intention. They plied him at once with questions about the location, the price, the size, and could not help doubting the wisdom of buying real estate in such a poor neighborhood.

"And see here, Timothy," said Will, "what about the trip you were gonna take? You don't look right yet, man, and as your doctor, friend, relative, adviser—I strongly recommend a sea voyage. At least take a trip to New York by water and get some of the cobwebs out of your brain before you settle down. Cobwebs staunch the flow of blood, and sometimes that's good and sometimes it's bad. A sluggish flow of blood in the brain—" He thumped his skull forebodingly with his large knuckles.

Timothy made a grimace. He couldn't explain why the mention of a sea voyage gave him a twinge of dismay, nor could he tell his good cousins sitting there so ample and wholesome by their fire why he couldn't bring himself to leave Charleston. He only knew that some force held him in stronger bonds than even Confederate loyalty warranted. So they sat for a while in an awkward silence while Will stroked the ears of the drowsy hound yawning against his knee and looked at his cousin with honest concern. Then he got up with a great *whoof* and opened all the windows again. As the fresh air poured in, Anna Maria steamed out of the room in dudgeon and Timothy made excuse to do the same.

Will, however, had put an idea into his head. He

would send Lena Whitlock on that sea voyage. He could afford it now, and going to bed that night he rolled the sweetmeat of benevolence under his tongue. But a day or so afterward he picked up the morning paper and there was Lena's obituary staring at him. This shock, this death, raised up a ghost to him, not her ghost but another's. It was no coincidence, he felt sure; with startling clarity he saw the trailing black dress beside him, the piled and shining hair, he heard on the morning air a faint creaking of old stays, familiar, ludicrous, and terrible. He had no doubt who had come out of her ashes and dealt him this rap.

The following week he sold the lot on which their house had stood and never went near it again. The street has run down anyway, he said aloud as he walked home from the bank where he had gone to deposit the money —the condition the city leaves the pavement in is a scandal! Why, you could break a leg just walking through it—

But he grieved for the shop, nevertheless, as he went prowling. The tips of his fingers remembered the cool marble of his pill-tile; whiffs of tar and turpentine from warehouses, nearly all smells, good or bad, rebuilt for him like magic the musty brown interior, the pointed arches, the live twinkle of the gas jet in the glass and china receptacles. As he sat on a post of the sea-wall and watched the gulls, golden-feathered in the bright, late sun like beings from another star, he began to think again about the solanum ointment and the lunar world he had caught sight of through the shop window. The effects of the ointment, he supposed, had been mild and partial because he had had so little of it left. Shall I buy the ingredients and mix some more? Shall I? But he had no accurate memory now of the proportions, and, besides, he knew intuitively that the old medico would not have committed the full secret to writing; like a canny cook, he would have left out some vital constituent of his recipe.

Perched on his post with one leg thrown over the top rail he stared across the harbor between the rise and fall of the gulls—should he try to find the Farr girl and persuade her to talk to him? But she had not wanted him to see the prescription at all, he remembered; it was only when he had refused her the solanum that she brought it out. She had the answers he needed, however, or some of them—perhaps the answer to his most gnawing doubt.

He jumped down from the post, walked to the corner, and took a streetcar to the Farrs' house.

The gray clapboards looked as blank and forbidding as he had remembered them. He paced up and down the sidewalk, trying to formulate a convincing excuse for ringing the doorbell. It proved singularly difficult—and God knew what unholy antics he might surprise her at. He bethought him of the corner grocer who had helped him out once before, and he strolled toward the shop to see what facts he could gather about this ambiguous household.

A kerosene lamp hanging from the low ceiling shed a lusterless twilight in the small dark shop. He heard the object of his quest before he saw her, in vigorous disputation with the proprietor. "Fifteen cents a *pound?* That's robbery! They're green anyway—" The grocer, melancholy but respectful, said, "But that's the price, Miss Lucy; cost me almost that much to buy them." "They're as hard as rocks." "Come now, they ain't as bad as all that—"

Leaning against the doorpost, Timothy blinked at this scene, so different from the one his imagination had painted. The mysterious Miss Farr, dickering and cajoling—it had never occurred to him that she shopped for supper like any other woman. She had driven a shrewd bargain, too, he suspected, because she was smiling as she picked up her bundles and jollying the proprietor. "Now, don't stand there looking at me like that. You give me the creeps. Muller, the gruesome greengrocer! I don't know why I trade here. Well, good night, all—"

Her darting walk carried her through the door so precipitately that she almost ran over Timothy. She stopped short; the level rays of the afternoon sun seemed to hold her suspended in the strong graphic colors of daytime. He took off his hat. "Good evening, Miss Farr."

"Well . . . this is a surprise. I didn't expect to run into you here."

"I was just out for a stroll and happened to see you. Allow me—" He took her package from her.

As she started up the street he fell in beside her, but

91

she went quickly along, keeping a little ahead as if not ready to consent to his company. Indeed, they were covering the short distance to her door with such speed that he was forced to plunge baldly into the matters that had brought him here. "I wanted to ask you—would you be so kind as to let me have a look at that prescription again? The one you brought to the shop."

He could feel her bantering mood slip from her. After a pause she said, "That wouldn't cure anything that ails you. You'd just better forget that visit."

"Forget our meeting? Don't ask too much of me. You can't just forget."

"You haven't got any supplies now."

"No, but I could scare up some. Curiosity, you know, is one of my besetting sins, and there's a lot going on in this town I'd like to know more about."

Already they had reached her gate. "I'd give up worrying about all that, if I were you. You were raised wrong —you're too scientific to learn anything." She reached for her bundle.

Timothy held on and as her hand touched his he held on to it too, supple, small-boned, the fingers ready, he guessed, to nip when the time came. "Don't go yet. There's something I think you can tell me. What about my sister?"

He felt her hand give a slight jerk of genuine surprise.

"Why—" She looked at him thoughtfully, perusing his mind with impersonal deliberation. Self-consciousness overtook him; he let loose his hold on her hand and the parcel. He couldn't go through with it, not to a girl in a plaid wool dress coming home from buying groceries at the corner. He couldn't even phrase his singular doubts. What did he want to ask: If Penelope was alive? If she was dead? If she was a ghost?

"Forgive me; what an absurd question. I'm still a little nervous, I suppose, since the fire. Please overlook this nonsense. We'll both forget our indiscretions, shall we?"

The gate-latch gave out a small, cool click under her hand. " 'Don't ask too much of me. You can't just forget.' " Her face puckered quizzically. "Good night—" The high, solid wooden gate closed behind her.

Timothy walked away feeling a slight discomfort next to his skin, as if from scratchy woolen clothing. Again he cursed his propensity for wild goose chases. If she knew the answers, he told himself crossly, she wouldn't share them for nothing—that had been obvious from the start. Well, he would go to headquarters; and he would come back a match for this aggravating hussy with her twopenny hocus-pocus. He would go to England after all; but not just yet.

In one of those spells like a warm breath down the neck of departing winter Timothy moved into the new house. Little effort was needed to make it habitable from his point of view. Soon after the purchase he had come across his erstwhile delivery-boy sitting cross-legged on a horse block in Queen Street; and beguiled by the deep blue of his overalls, the rich butternut of

his skin, Timothy forgot Pollo's idleness and unrelia-
bility and hired him on the spot as his general servant.
A colored man came in and calcimined the walls salmon
pink, which gave them, Timothy thought, a handsome
and worldly air. Anna Maria sniffed because there were
no conveniences, but Timothy had the outhouse cleaned
and neatly repaired, and the cistern, he pointed out,
would provide him, via a pump in the kitchen, with
more water than he could possibly use. He stood off
Anna Maria's well-meant offers to make curtains for
him and left the windows bare, but he accepted from
Will a fine deerskin rug, evidence of his cousin's prowess.

On the first evening he spent in the house he got
himself something to eat in the new clean kitchen. He
sat with his feet on the wood range and tilted his chair
back; he dipped his toast in his tea and it tasted hot and
sweet. Freedom, he found, could be dizzying and cosy
at the same time.

His study was still in confusion, so when he had piled
the tea-things in the sink he went up to the front room
on the third floor which he had chosen as his bedroom
because of the water-view. Before the fire stood a treas-
ure, a high-backed armchair with a curved and carven
frame, close cousin to the pair Penelope and Mr. Dombie used to occupy by the dining-room fire. He had
pounced on it in the secondhand shop from which he
had furnished his house; among the dusty bedposts,
tables, towel racks, bidets, sitting in a haphazard circle
of sociability, it had reared up dignified and familiar,
its deep-tufted horsehair upholstery very nourishing to

94

some obscure sense of privation. He had had it carted home at once to ensure his possession of it.

Now he sat down in it with an air of triumph and stretched his legs to the blaze he had kindled in the open fireplace—for this outmoded dwelling had not progressed so far as coal grates. But his self-importance quickly ran out. He had never stayed alone in a house before; his parents, Penelope, the Golightlys, had hung round him like parlor curtains whose absence left him feeling draftily exposed. Even Pollo's presence would have helped, but the boy went home every night when his work was done. The bedroom seemed cheerless in spite of the salmon-pink walls. Queer noises in the yard below disturbed him; he made a trip downstairs and applied one eye to a crack in the back door, but it was only the brindled cat crunching the fish-heads Pollo had thrown out after dinner. "Scat, Grimalkin!" Timothy cried, dashing a pail of water over her. With a snarl she streaked off into the black yard.

He went upstairs again to the drumming of his own footsteps against the closed doors on either hand. The empty rooms oppressed him, waiting behind their blank doors. He caught himself thinking, Sister would have had this one, Mr. Dombie that. Unexpectedly he grieved for the clutter of the old house, the books, the plump sofa modestly skirted with fringe that touched the floor, the crowded pictures—even for *The Last Judgment.*

The armchair by his fire was comfortable enough, however, and he slouched in it, his hands clasped

95

behind his head, looking rather like a bat if the truth were told, with the dark hair about his face, and his thin arms making sharp black angles on either side. Presently he took the bankbook from the table beside him and looked over it. Although his purchases had eaten a hole in his fortune, as he liked to call it, a substantial balance still showed in his savings account. The figures produced a comforting warmth in his middle region. . . . Confound it! I forgot to take out any fire insurance! Imagine my not even thinking of it. . . . But he felt somehow that there was no point. Well, he had certainly been psychic about paying the premium on the other house, he remembered a little smugly. Or had some hovering presence cynically guided him in this act?

The night passed peacefully except for a nightmare he had about the shop. He stood outside in a drowning rain looking through the window; the gas at the end of the long pipe winked wanly on the shelf bottles, the pot-bellied stove was cold and black, unfilled prescriptions for desperate ills had drifted against the counter, the little wafer-thin weights of his apothecary's scales lay scattered on the floor like wet leaves. Someone else, someone he couldn't distinguish, clumped about with queer, uneven footfalls, one soft, one hard and heavy, as if the owner wore a metallic shoe. He was rattling the crucibles and long-necked bottles, brewing a lethal draught which Timothy had somehow had a hand in. Choked with horror at his own complicity he tried to reach the door, but the deluge that was sweeping everything away dragged at his legs; the shop came loose and floated out of his reach, he woke up swimming and thrashing in hideous distress.

In the daytime life went more cheerfully. Timothy and Pollo weeded the dreary strip of yard running from the house to the front gate and dug in some manure from the livery stable. He did not know yet what he would plant in the garden; he lived from day to day waiting to see what the next would show forth.

The neighborhood into which he had moved began to interest him. He had passed through this street a number of times, but without seeing much above the pavement. Resting from his digging, he leaned on the front gate and looked along the block. The small, unimpressive houses seemed strung together by a thread of sheer tension. Negroes and whites lived side by side, with brown faces predominating, but race had nothing to do with the jostling, irreligious gait that characterized the quarter. The cookshop leaned sidewise and shoved against the colored church with the subhuman perversity of wood and tin; and beside the curb of the unpaved roadway the grass had already begun its crawling assault on brick and stone.

The vendors who called their wares along the street made Timothy's housekeeping easy. As he hung over the gate a fat colored woman came by with her barrow, selling oysters. Timothy sent Pollo to the kitchen for a pan and engaged her in conversation while he waited. Did she live in this part of town, he wanted to know. Near by, she said, but the noncommittal syllables scarcely

97

constituted an assent. He had just moved here, Timothy explained—an unnecessary remark; she would have known all about him from the moment he had come with the keys to look at the house. Her glance was watchful; not hostile, simply without trust. "Well, your oysters look fine and fresh," he said, pumping friendliness into his voice. He took the pan from the returning Pollo and held it out. "I'll take a quart today."

The oysterwoman, without response, dipped her ladle into the cedar bucket in the barrow and poured the exact measure into the outstretched pan. Timothy paid her and sent Pollo to the corner store for a piece of ice. "Stop by again; I'm very fond of oysters. You have a new customer now."

A flick of white showed between the woman's lids as she spread a newspaper over the bucket to keep the sun off. She had no intention, he saw, of giving him a nod, a beck, a nail-paring, that might be used against her should he prove to have come here under the wrong auspices. Without a "Good day" she picked up the handles of her barrow and rolled fleshily away over the flagstones.

On Sunday he went to the Golightlys', who had hospitably given him a standing invitation to Sunday dinner. As he sat in the parlor he could hear a stifled argument going on in the dining room where Will had gone to mix the toddies. Anna Maria whispered something he couldn't catch, but Will could never more than half throttle his natural roar, so Timothy distinctly heard: "Oh, you are better at this sort of thing than I am." Then Anna Maria, more sharply: "Not I. He's *your* relation—you'll have to tackle him."

Timothy stalled his rocking chair and listened. The Golightlys, with the good taste often shown by clumsy people, had withheld comment on his failure to go to church since the fire, though Timothy had been in constant dread of the day when they would mention it. He braced himself and tried hurriedly to assemble some logic for his skirting the church doors. Wasn't it generally understood that lost souls dared not go to church? But he was not quite sure about his soul; and if it was lost he was getting on surprisingly well without it.

Presently Will, having drawn the short straw apparently, came out alone to "tackle" him. When they had each had a swallow of the toddy he plunged in. "I declare, you're looking right sassy these days, Tim, in spite of Father Time. Well, I dare say we all look older, but you've just turned thirty-five, and oughtn't to mind— Look here, old man, you better do something about your hair." He softened his remark with a solicitous grin. "Black or white, green or grizzled, I don't care which, but just make up your mind to one. You can't go trotting round town like a piebald pony—"

Timothy passed his hand dreamily over his head. In his relief at having escaped the subject of church, he took his cousin's frankness amiably. "That's so. It must look a little odd. But I don't seem to mind being piebald and I'm the only one it matters to."

When they joined Anna Maria at table Will gave her a wink no one could have missed; and the meal went off in cousinly affability. Anna Maria was a large-boned, kindly woman not unlike her husband, and their daughters were built to scale. Timothy found the noisy, hearty Golightlys in their big dog-ridden house a little tiring and returned with pleasure to the narrow proportions of his own rooms, which did not make him feel dwarfish. On Monday morning, however, he stopped in at the Palace Shaving Saloon and had his hair cut to the gray line. He couldn't escape a pang at the sight of his raven locks on the floor around the barber's chair; still, in his present queer state of mind he had ceased to anticipate either youth or age. . . .

His cropped head made him more than ever a marked man. People looked at him sidelong; women, hanging out of windows in his street, fell silent as he passed. The horrors of his experience had set him off from the common touch, and this realization fed his craving for privacy and anonymity.

A few of his old customers began to seek him out, poor whites and colored folk largely, but his supply of roots and herbs had gone up in smoke with the other stocks of his apothecary's trade. They gave him, however, an idea for his well-prepared garden beds. The season had passed for gathering roots; this was the time to move plants in from the woods, to make unguents and tinctures from their leaves, so he took several jaunts into the country and nosed around with a basket and trowel. He and Pollo set out his cullings in neat rows along the walls of his little strip.

Coming home from an excursion one evening he

found himself nervously exhilarated, as if the kitchen physic he carried had started to work on him. He looked about with heightened sensitivity at the life burgeoning in the quarter to which he had moved; its denizens, he concluded, belonged to a vegetable empire, their sap rose instantly in response to the warm time of the year. Cows, goats, chickens, milled in the streets in defiance of city ordinances; blows and curses sounded in the saloon, feet scuttled through the twilight, and shutters banged to. The pushcarts of the vendors streaked the dusk with the flame and soot of their lightwood flares. The constant movement raised a film of dust down the middle of the roadway.

Walking in the crowd with his basket Timothy felt the contagion all around him. It was as if a touch at his elbow, a word at his ear, would bring this flighty element within his grasp. Before his empty house he paused, for he had an instant impression of some dissonance in its welcome, some invasion during his absence. For a few moments he stood under the lamp-post near his gate, feeling slightly sheepish at his unwillingness to leave its comforting refulgence. He glanced down at the yellow circle of light laid almost explicitly at his feet, and saw that it enclosed a little slough, a low place along the curbstone where rain collected. Stamped on the black mud the print of a cloven foot had filled with water and lay there golden in the falling light.

Timothy took a second look, then he went diffidently up the path to his door. Not a lock had been disturbed,

not even the stuffy air of the closed rooms seemed dis-
arranged by this intrusion.

The next morning he went into the yard to set out
his plants. All the time he was working over them
curiosity tugged at his elbow, and presently he dropped
his trowel and walked out to the lamppost. In the clear
light of morning the footprint was distinctly there, but
no longer golden, a drying footprint of what might
easily be Mrs. Sweegan's cow. The lowings of this
animal frequently woke him up in the morning, Mrs.
Sweegan's cowshed being against his house. "But," he
said aloud, "if Mrs. Sweegan's cow's footprint can look
like the Devil's, couldn't the Devil's footprint look like a
cow's?" From what he had seen of Mrs. Sweegan she
was not a person of imagination who would lend him
her cow to see if its foot would fit the discarded slipper.

That evening Timothy sat by his hearth dispirited in
spite of himself. The weather continued warm and
enervating. He had let the fire die down; the big iron
kettle that was his hot-water supply hissed faintly in the
ashes. His shoes lay parrytoed on the hearth where he
had kicked them, and unable to concentrate on his
reading he sat and listened to the silence, wishing it
were time to go to bed. But silence never lasted long
in this neighborhood; a harsh cry broke out somewhere
down the street, followed by a stillness just as singular.
He raised the window and listened: nothing. Whoever
uttered the cry roused no interest, no succor. He went
downstairs several times to investigate noises in the back

yard, but his lifted lamp showed only brickbats and dead leaves on the bare ground.

Coming back from his last descent, he thought he heard a noise in the empty room opposite his own. Plucking up his nerve, he opened the door and looked in. Nothing out of the ordinary greeted his eye except for a lacy semicircle of soot around the empty fireplace. As he stood there more soot rattled down the throat of the chimney; a chimney swift perhaps—he tried to remember when the swifts came south. The rattle ceased, and he returned to his room across the hall leaving both doors open behind him. As he crossed the threshold Will's deerskin rose a little on the floor to meet him, the dun flanks heaved with a panting life; Timothy clutched the lamp, which almost slipped from his fingers—then the skin fell dead again and lay sleek on the boards. The draft from the open doors and windows which had given it a similitude of breath petered out, whining.

Timothy set the lamp on the center table and lowered the sash. Then he planted a chair on the deerskin and sat down on it to trim his lamp, which was smoking this evening, owing to Pollo's inattentive ministrations. Scarcely had he seated himself when a scratching began on the roof, a padding as of foot-soles, a rattle of loosened plaster down the tiles. Once more he raised the window and leaned out, craning to see past the edge of the dormer; but all that his narrow angle of vision disclosed was the bell-like curve of the roof fading into the darkness. As he drew his head in there came a sudden fall of soot in the next room, a quick rustle, a felt presence. He stood perfectly still facing the window, unable to summon the force to cross the hall again. He could hear each of his heartbeats, loud as a leaf falling in the quiet of night.

When he turned round he saw a woman standing in the door of his room, her skirts still blowing with the immediacy of her arrival. She was small and strangely dressed; her skin had a curious deep flush, and a trace of the same color seemed to stain her long yellow hair. Dark smudges encircled her eyes, or perhaps the great tawny fringe falling over her forehead gave them their smoky look. She came a little farther in on delicate bare feet.

Timothy said baldly, "Who are you?"

"A visitor," she said, "just calling on a person of importance who has moved into the neighborhood. Natural, isn't it?" Her smiling mouth had in its fullness both cruelty and the capacity for enjoyment. "And this narrow, leafy house, I've always liked it—it's my kind of house as well as your kind." The lamplight shone in her eyes and died out again as they moved about the room. "You've made yourself a nice retreat up here on the top floor. You imagined you'd get away from everybody, didn't you?"

Timothy sank against the window sill, gripping the ledge with both hands. He thought of the three-story drop to the ground below and stayed where he was. Besides, among his churning emotions he felt the strong

104

bite of curiosity. "Perhaps I was hoping for privacy," he said after a moment; "but I don't know why you should come after me. I'm not a person of importance—" He snatched up mediocrity like an invisible cloak and flung it round him. "I'm merely a bush-rabbit pharmacist—"

"Not a person of importance? Why, the whole town has been talking about you since the lamentable death of your sister and her friend from which you miraculously escaped." Her sarcastic smile parted her thin red lips again. "People are puzzled about you, they have a feeling in their bones that the burning of your house was not an accident."

Her words thudded against Timothy's breastbone. He swallowed and said, "I don't know what you mean."

"Shall we go into it a little further?"

"There's nothing to go into." He drew himself up and was uncomfortably aware of a falsity, a bed-slat absurdity, in his bearing.

"Well, you're a little careless with fire, it seems to a mere outsider. To go off and leave that—book burning, and all those papers around. But you always had a fine Promethean way with matches and combustibles, if I remember your dossier correctly."

Tall as he pulled and stretched himself, Timothy could no longer cage within his ribs the actuality he had spent these last weeks ignoring. He turned as red as his visitor and sank against the sill again.

"Yes . . . it's true. I wished their deaths. I felt them there on my back all the time, a load that pressed me down so all my juice ran out. I had to get them off some-how."

His visitor was enjoying herself. She gave a light crowing laugh, surprising, as if a canary crowed. "And disposed of them in handsome style! But I must warn you that you don't get an encumbrance off your back by such easy and primitive means. It will simply shift its form. 'Perpetual in perpetual change.' " And she took another step into the room.

He was struggling to collect himself, to recall if his books had given any practical advice about the taming of hags and apparitions, but the creatures flew and batted about in his mind in too distracting a company. He could only think, the trip to England doesn't seem to be necessary.

Timothy rose from his crouching position and also took a step toward the middle of the room with a sort of hopeless scheme of keeping the table between them. As if she read his thought the hag came soundlessly up to the table and placed her finger-tips on the marble top. The lamp sent up a furious small eruption of smoke at her approach and by the light that came through the blackened chimney he saw she was younger than the word "hag" implied. Not a wrinkle marked her strange glistering skin; she was neither young nor old. She smiled slightly, her tongue between her teeth, a frank smile of hunger and anticipation.

A Bible! Timothy thought wildly, if you read the Bible backward . . . But he had burned his up, of course! His tottery self-confidence collapsed in ruin. He dodged past the table; sheer desperation carried him into the hall, he plunged down the stairs, stumbling, slipping, his ankles twisting under him. But when he reached the black hole at the bottom he knew he had not come alone; a light burden hung at his back. He sprang forward in a shuddering revulsion at the touch of its cold small fingers like a caterpillar on his neck. Bursting through the door somehow, he raced down the path.

He was without volition now except the frantic urge to get away, to shake his burden by speed—the only idea left in his disintegrated mind. Sometimes they seemed to stand still while the spaced circles of lamplight rushed at them and splashed them with flecks of yellow foam. His stockinged feet thudded softly on the pavement; at his ear he heard a high thin whistling like the wind, or like the hag's breath coming faintly through her teeth.

Not a living creature stirred—if indeed they still traveled the territory of the living. The fear of Retribution parched his tongue. Far down the church aisle of his memory he heard the familiar denunciations; the sound of sin beat down from scowling pulpits and rattled in his hollow head. Trees lined his road, their bare limbs straining and streaming back in the hideous wind; prophets like bass-horns shouted after him, but he was too fleet for these evangelical threats. Faster than sound he ran ahead of their brassy syllables—

By this time his lungs were bursting. The hope of escape strangled and died. He felt the roadway soft under him like an unpaved street. . . . But even this

107

shred of consciousness flowed away in the wind as he lurched, fell, and gave in at last to the luxury of defeat.

The shred of consciousness tightened about his brain again and squeezed it once or twice. How weak our hold is on time, a voice seemed to be saying; and truly he had no idea whether hours, days or years had passed over him since . . . But now space moved in about him, black and cramping. Space was rectangular, he discovered, with narrow chinks of brightness, the very shape of a tomb. Above his face as he lay on his back a slab of blackness pressed down. In his utter deflation of mind and body he rested content to be a corpse, until suddenly consciousness coiled round him again and gave a venomous squeeze—for if it was a tomb he was alive in it. He twisted on his side, started up, staggered about, and struck a vertical object, tallish, bony, and slick to the touch. The rectangle tipped and swayed. . . . Then the sheer force of his grip on the upright seemed to steady the rocking walls, which settled with a jolt to their proper orientation. It was his own room that enclosed him, the hard ribby frame of his armchair that his fingers clutched.

He fell into it; the familiar twang of the springs under the horsehair more enchanted his ears than all the harps of heaven. He lay back gasping, trying to quell the riot in his body, the pained protest of his blood vessels, engorged by fear and horror.

At last he stirred out of his thick exhaustion, stumbled across the room, and opened the shutters. A deep shadow leaned out from the house into the garden and pointed toward the east; it must be about four o'clock of a brisk spring afternoon.

His clothes were covered with dust, his sock soles worn through. He turned and crept downstairs, creaking in every joint. The house was still; looking into the back yard, he saw Pollo dozing in the wheelbarrow under a tree. "Pollo! wake up, boy—" His throat muscles, he found, were stiff as if from screaming.

Pollo turned his head. He looked at his employer with blank face, covering his private impression.

"Come on in and heat up the kettle."

Luckily the kettle was on the stove. Pollo carried it upstairs and made a fire in the bedroom. Timothy dragged his tin tub to the hearth and squatted in it while Pollo basted his painful limbs with hot soapy water. A hot bath being miraculously a tonic for the soul as well as the body, these little simplicities gradually restored him, he began to pluck up heart. When he had dressed he went into the room across the hall and looked about. It was tightly shuttered, but by the stream of light from the hall door he saw the fan of soot before the fireplace scarred over with marks like lettering. The cipher was beyond his translation; only the sole of a hurrying bare foot had left an imprint in a universal script.

He drank some black coffee, went out to the street, and sat down on the curbstone. People would think this queer—but if you had attracted the attentions of a hag you needn't worry any longer about making yourself conspicuous, and this reflection brought him some comfort. He had to consider what to do now. From where he sat he could see the dormer window of his own room twinkling above the wall as the sun struck fire from the rich burgundy of the tiles, and his heart bled for his dream of living there. But where could he go?

The Golightlys' house he rejected immediately; the bedrooms had open fireplaces with particularly wide chimneys. Besides, he shrank from the humiliation of revealing his plight to them. Nor was there anyone else whom he would have know of it—Lucy least of all. There remained the streets, with such safety as they might bring. He thirsted for more information on the habits of nocturnal spirits, and cursed his lack of foresight in burning up his library with his sister. Wretchedly pondering his dilemma, he sat on until dark.

He went home after a while and freed Pollo, who was tugging at the leash, and carefully locked up the house. He got rid of an hour or so on a park bench; then the lights of a saloon down the block flared companionably. He sipped his whisky slowly, and for a while the chatter and the mere closeness of human bodies soothed and diverted him. But presently he noticed that no one joined him at his table; he began to feel that eyes moved quickly away when he met them, that a whisper went hither and yon among the leaning heads. He grew more and more edgy, sitting like a long bolster against the wall. They could hardly know of his disgrace—but he was no longer any judge of what could happen and what could not. He paid for his drinks and left, aware that he went in jerks like a man distraught.

The streets had emptied. From the spaces between the houses eddies of darkness flowed out, bringing danger and his own conviction of defeat to overwhelm him. Now physical fatigue sapped his limbs of all substance. He tried to rally himself: Where was his courage? But this was not the day for it, he thought; at any rate, he could see no escape. His guilt was too plain. He went back and let himself into his house.

The light of his lamp wavered on the walls as he mounted the stairs. The house was quiet as a tomb, his room empty. He set the lamp on the table and looked about him thoughtfully for a few minutes. Then he dragged the washstand over to the fireplace and pushed it against the opening. He locked the door across the hall and, returning to his room, locked his own door. Then he sat down in the armchair to wait.

The lamp he had brought from downstairs had been better tended than his own and its light burned clear and steady. The usual night noises came up from below, and once he heard a cat, Grimalkin, no doubt, mew petulantly. Putting his head back, he stared up at the ceiling, his ears straining for noises on the roof, but no sounds came down to him except the wind in the trees, sighing and soughing in a pleasant, familiar melancholy. The muscles in the back of his neck began to hurt, and he bowed his head on his chest for a moment to rest them.

When he came to, the cool challenge of morning was in the air and he felt in all his body the divine refreshment of a night's sleep. Incredulous he ran to the window and opened the shutters; the salt-tasting air rushed in, from the little hood of his dormer he saw the innocent blue water and absorbed through the pores of his skin the early damp rising from the ground.

His numbed brain began to stir again. He began to think of ways to amend his situation. He would take steps. He would go ask the advice of Maum Rachel. When he had breakfasted he put some bread and cheese in his pocket and walked several blocks to the end of the car line.

He found the driver turning the car on the turntable while the horse sidled before it. Robinson was an old acquaintance, so Timothy walked through to the front platform and rode beside him. They exchanged the dry facts they always exchanged, and these unalterable platitudes, this relaxed and disconnected talk, steadied the shifty universe. The streets quivered with released energies; like the spring shrubs, people put on green and purple over their winter drab. Robinson was so wholesomely common, his face so blue with morning stubble, that Timothy could not but marvel at the richness of a Creation which fathered forth the incongruous persons of his nocturnal visitor and the kindly carman.

The marvel of the steam engine never failed to excite him, but today its noble pace seemed sluggish to his changed sense of speed. The country rolled past at an easy gait, and after a short time a sign saying "Otranto" dawdled by close to the window and stopped. Timothy got out.

The stop was a mere shed at a crossroads; the locomotive shook its bell like a brass mane, huffed, puffed, and jangled away, leaving him alone in the road. Silence surged in its wake like an inward-curling plume and disposed of its fussy sociability. But the journey before him had to be undertaken in loneliness; it was only thanks to this untenanted countryside that he needn't go like King Saul disguised and at night. He started to walk briskly, for the plantation to which Maum Rachel had returned to spend her old age was a good three miles away.

Spring in these woods was not delicate but violent; the mustard-green fuzz of the oaks outbrazened the other greens, the swamp maples dashed red flecks against the pure sky; after being winter-pent in the spare twigs, leaves rushed up into being—no time to be lost. They glittered, tossed, demanded attention, their sheen made the spring shadows blacker. Medicinal plants sent up dank noon smells from the ditchbank at Timothy's feet. Red man's, white man's, black man's magic—they rose beside him, they ran down the gray ravelings of the moss . . . he was astonished that he should ever have considered going abroad to look for answers.

The high-pitched yelping of two or three mangy curs announced his arrival as he turned into a narrow tunnel that led through the underbrush to Maum Rachel's cabin. She came to the door and looked out, a tall woman with a regal carriage, shading her old eyes, which were milky with cataracts. She and Timothy greeted each other with a sentiment, a sentimentality even, held strictly in leash; Maum Rachel could have burst into a high screaming, and Timothy in his present state of nerves might almost have done the same. But they kept their balance, and stood gravely still, their hands clasped.

Had she heard about the fire, Timothy wanted to know. To be sure she had—what a time, what a calamitation! "I have to talk to you," he said looking at the colored children streaming toward the stranger like flies to the molasses jug.

Maum Rachel raised her arm with a swift gesture of doom and the children scattered. "Come dis side, suh," she said, walking stiffly down the steps, and led the way across the little clearing.

The big house had burned long since by some feckless accident and only a few jagged fragments stood above the brick foundations. The front steps came out from under the mat of honeysuckle that had covered the ruin, and on these Timothy sat down and told his story while Maum Rachel stood before him wrapped in her dark brown silence. Her nose was flat but not thick—the bridge had two sharply carven angles where it sloped away on either side, and in her long sunken cheeks it made one plane with forehead and chin. It was like a ceremonial mask—which Timothy used to think she put on or off; she was sometimes one person and sometimes another. He did not mention his guilt in the deaths of his sister and Mr. Dombie, knowing she would assume this from what followed.

The implications, he saw, troubled Maum Rachel's

moral sense no whit. Danger threatened her foster child; her partisanship was single-minded. All those night creatures were bad now, she assured him, boo-daddies, boo-hags, plat-eyes, were raging round. Lavinia Coaxum over by Goose Crick had been ridden forty nights straight. She had wasted away to a shadow until somebody sat by her bed and caught the hag in a bottle with a needle in it. The needle stuck the hag and killed it, and Lavinia had gotten well. Who were his enemies? she wanted to know.

Timothy spoke frankly. "It must be Sister Penny, Maum Rachel. She has a motive, God knows."

Maum Rachel shook her turbaned head. Hags are human people, not ghosts. They get a holt on you by stealing something that belongs to you—a lock of your hair, most likely, or a nail paring.

Timothy stroked his shorn head nervously, while he tried to remember if anyone bore him malice. The barbers at the Palace Shaving Saloon had no motive for picking up his hair, furthermore they were excluded by reason of sex. "For a long time I had a notion Sister was still alive somewhere; but that doesn't make sense either."

"Miss Penny never did have no patience sence she was little. If she love you or hate you she'd be at it till Jedgment. I don't feel her roun' nowheres."

"A strange young lady named Miss Farr did come into the shop looking for nightshade. I suspect she dabbles in witchcraft, but she had no reason to be my enemy—"

Maum Rachel considered the puzzle with pursed lips.

115

The hag, she said, must have gotten a holt on him some way.

"Maum Rachel, she was so curious-looking!"

"Sho'—sho'. Mos' likely she done slip her skin an' lef' it behin' de do' somewheres. If you kin fin' de skin, Mas' Timity, an' fill it full o' red pepper—"

"I couldn't! Besides, she seemed to be wearing it—fortunately—and wearing it rather well, come to think of it. It was just an unusual color."

Well, he had better sprinkle some pepper about before she came again, in the chimney and on the floor. Red pepper was mighty aggravating to hags without their skins.

"But there must be something else I can do, Maum Rachel," he said, feeling this remedy a bit too simple.

The only true cure was to catch the hag in a bottle as Lavinia Coaxum's mother had, and jab her with a needle. He must get a friend to sit up with him while he slept and watch for her.

But if Timothy had no enemies, neither had he any friends, he discovered, at least none he could call on to perform so delicate a service. Besides, it took quickness and skill. Pollo was too young and would bolt at the mere suggestion.

"I uster could ketch hag befo' me yeye gone back on me, but me old man hab anoder wife yonder 'cross Goose Crick an' she put cunjer on me 'tel I can't see good."

"There must be some other way."

Maum Rachel covered her face with her long sinewy

hands and studied and studied. Well, yes—other things worked sometimes. There was a strong charm she could make. It would take goofer dust—graveyard dust—stump water, and . . . well, different things. If he would lead her to the graveyard she would try.

The air was thick with pollen when they went through the green tunnel toward the road. Maum Rachel leant on Timothy's arm and felt the path before her with her crooked stick. They talked devoutly of old times, of Timothy's parents, of the happy days before the War, of his dead sister and brother, working on each other's feelings with humor for half-forgotten pranks and with sorrow for these remembered deaths.

The Negro graveyard lay not far from the house. A grove of oaks enclosed it like a Romanesque crypt, the thick, squat trunks and the flat arched boughs seemed cast into a deep sleep by their own shade; the hum of innumerable insect-wings came from its depths like the very sound of sleep. Once inside, Maum Rachel dropped Timothy's arm and made her way about with certainty in her bent limbs. She talked to herself in a low voice and sometimes she stooped and picked up this or that. On the simple mounds about them a few personal belongings had been set, a mug, an oil lamp, the medicine used in the last illness, for which the dead might have further need. A new grave near Timothy's feet held a dish of peas and rice half-eaten.

Maum Rachel did not touch any possession of the dead. Timothy, however, made no attempt to spy upon her; he leaned against a tree trunk without thought;

only his nerves vibrated to the implications gathered in this deserted spot. All that was ambiguous about life, the half-seen, the underheard, beat against his eyeballs, and his fingers dug into the deep-cleft bark of the oak with a drowning grasp. The activities of his mind were shriveled away by a childish hope of succor. An inconsecutive rustling, the occasional snapping of a loud twig, kept him aware of Maum Rachel's still hunt.

She appeared suddenly at his elbow, startling him out of nothingness; in that lulled light her skin had the gray shimmer of black stone. As they dragged their slow way back along the road, Maum Rachel did not tell him what she held knotted in her soiled apron; instead she diverted him with tales of the ghosts that sometimes flew out of the graveyard like a flock of buzzards, of the adversities that had befallen people in the neighborhood because of cunjers thrown on them; by this same blasted pine she had seen a calf going through the woods one night with his head cut off. . . .

Timothy listened with the old enthrallment. His experiences of the last two days acquired depth and texture from these tales and others like them which he had heard with faith and a shivering delight at Maum Rachel's knee. His years in the shop seemed short and brittle, the advances of scientific learning looked pretentious and naïve against the ancient, instinctive wisdom that welled in this little pocket in the underbrush, shielded from a civilization that corrupts the instincts.

It would take her a while, Maum Rachel said when

118

they reached her cabin, to fix things up. Mas' Timity had better go for a little walk.

"I have to catch the evening train—" Timothy looked at his watch.

If he would come back by dusk-dark, Maum Rachel thought she would have everything ready.

Timothy walked over to the creek toward which the big house had faced. At the end of what had been an *allée* he stopped to admire the view, the placid dark blue water edged with cresslike plants. His stomach suddenly gave him a stab of reproach, and he took his lunch from his pocket. A white gleam in the growth at his feet caught his eye; he pulled away the vines and found a statue, broken into sections, from the old garden. In spite of the defacement of time he easily recognized the goddess Diana. She looked very chaste indeed after the visions he had been seeing—her limbs and narrow flanks youthful and untried. "You couldn't do me any good in the fix I'm in," he said explanatorily; "you're not in my mythology." And sitting down on her flat little huntress's belly, he ate his bread and cheese.

A magical calm descended on the water with the descending sun. Pearly colors glossed over the surface of the creek. A flock of coots flew in and circled low over his still head with a wooden creaking of wings. They struck the calm water in a wild urgence, slicing deep into the darkness underneath, and vanished, full of anxious nighttime talk, into the sedge. Timothy felt his heart bared in some physical sense to their anxiety, to all the impounded fear and loss that underlay the world.

Diana began to prove as hard of muscle as rumor reported, and he got up and went down to the creekside and drank deeply. When he returned to Maum Rachel's cabin he found her ready for him. A mule and a farm wagon stood by the door; her husband had come home and would take Timothy to the train. Maum Rachel drew Timothy aside and slipped two balls, each sewed up in cloth, into his hand. He must hide them in the chimneys; she had made them extra strong to keep all evil spirits away from his rooftree.

Timothy gave her some money, which was not a payment but a pledge of their relationship, a distinction they both understood. "Gawd bless you, Mas' Timity; I gwine ter pray for you."

"Thank you, Maum Rachel—thank you," he said with a gratitude and affection untroubled by any sense of incongruity. Devoutly he grasped the familiar old hands and pressed them. Then he mounted to the wagon seat and drove down the dark road. The ambling motion of the loose-wheeled wagon made the cunjer balls in his pocket bump gently against his hip. He knew he should be ashamed of his descent to such moonshine, but his meeting with Maum Rachel had given him a peace he had not felt for two long days and nights. The country noises as they plodded through the gray evening still carried an inimical sound; the sudden wild shrilling of peepers from the ditch, and their equally sudden cessation, still seemed the voices of alarm in the earth, the evil under its wrinkled skin. But now, he thought, perhaps some of them would be on his side.

It was late when he got back to his house. He went straight to the kitchen, took a pepper-cruet from the shelf, and climbed to the third floor. He fortified both chimneys with the charms and a liberal sprinkling of red pepper, moving the washstand from his hearth to do a thorough job in his own room. He doubted if a mere washstand would have afforded him protection in any case. Nevertheless, he pushed it back against the opening just for luck.

When he had eaten some supper he returned to his room, locked the door, and sat down in his armchair. He considered going to bed, but his faith was not quite strong enough to allow him to risk being caught in his nightshirt— He started up with a wild notion that if he *was* in his nightshirt a lady might hesitate to come in, and he half-unbuttoned his coat; but immediately he realized the folly of hoping for any such reticence on her part, and sank back in his chair again. This time he kept on his stout walking shoes.

The country air had made him drowsy and he dozed in spite of himself. The sudden clank of metal on wood roused him. He sat up and grasped the arms of his chair; then he saw that the key on the inside of his bedroom door had fallen to the floor. As he stared rigid with denial, a little spurt of rosy dust came through the keyhole. Like smoke above a flame it spun, became a feather, a column, a cloud; but slowly, irrefutably it solidified before his eyes into the shape of the hag.

He looked at her dumfounded. "How—did you get in?" he stammered, though he had just watched her entrance. The hag took something from her mouth and, gliding to the fireplace, she put it on the end of the mantel.

With a deep shudder Timothy gave up his foolish hopes and did not move away at her approach. He was too defeated even to stand in the presence of a lady; he merely glared at her along the marble top of the washstand. The hag's bright lips parted in one of her scoffing smiles. "Did you really think you could keep me out by that mish-mash of Maum Rachel's?" She nodded toward the chimney.

"Mish-mash?" Timothy looked at her stupefied. "But I thought of course—I thought you believed in magic!"

"You are a feeler, my dear man, not a thinker. And all your reading did you little good if you don't know that the world you are touching is hieratical. My art is well above Maum Rachel's simple skill. My means of operation are too varied for her."

"Who are you?" Timothy asked, emboldened by hopelessness.

"Whoever you like." She shrugged, and the shadow deepened in the little hollow of her throat. "I use all sorts of names—you can take your choice. I can also assume a great many shapes, though not as many as the higher orders of witches. Among other things I can hold

a cat bone in my mouth"—she touched the object she
had laid on the mantel—" and go through a very small
crevice, a keyhole, for instance."

Timothy looked at the keyhole and back at his visitor. "Who are you?" he said again. "You must be somebody—you must have a real name."

"My 'real' name? Nonsense! If I had a real name, I
wouldn't tell it. Call me anything you like. Let's see—
you may call me Sinkinda. That's a witch name that
will suit your romantic fancy, I imagine." And her dark-
ringed eyes sparkled with malice.

"These orders of Evil, I find them very confusing,"
said Timothy, aggrieved. "It's disquieting not to know
where you stand. In pharmacy you have a formula, you
can weigh your ingredients to the smallest grain, but in
matters of superstition—"

"Superstition? Evil is a religion where I come from.
You are taken in by yokel's words."

Timothy could not help showing that he was scandal-
ized. "Evil certainly isn't a real religion; I know better.
Why, it has no churches, no saints, and no hymnbooks.
I am a religious man—or was," he added ruefully.

"So you imagine. But do you really think you can
separate superstition from religion? What you need is
a good stiff course in comparative theology instead of
those dreary sermon books you read. Or did," she
mocked him. "The truth is you aren't real either; everything about you is a little pseudo—you're a character
out of the Gothic revival."

This gibe galled Timothy immoderately. "Me—

Gothic? How ridiculous! I'm a middling honest pharmacist, a Christian gentleman, and fond of reading.
That's all."

"You're a dabbler in medievalism, a part-time monk,
and stuffed with religiosity. There's no real construc-
tion behind that perpendicular façade."

Timothy scarcely knew how to defend himself
against these charges. Could he properly use a Christian's weapons in his state of disgrace? He fell back on an
old prop in times of doubt. "If Sister were here she'd
be a match for your sophistries. Her faith was sturdier
than mine; I'd like to hear you tell her that magic
isn't evil and the Christian faith not the only good."

Sinkinda seated herself on the arm of a rocking chair,
riding it like a sidesaddle. Her skirt of hunter's green
fell in appropriate loops, and indeed it was cut like a
riding habit, he saw, though the stuff was supple and
airy. "Good . . . Evil . . . what do you know about them?
Humans are stupid not to believe in the old gods—or
devils, if you prefer. There is Evil in the world, I assure
you, not dreamed of in Sister's second-rate decalogue,
though she knew more than she let on. You have to have
wit, and especially the right kind of faith, to understand
it. Of course there are plenty of people who do. More
of your friends believe in magic than you suspect."

Timothy was forced to assent to this; yet a sense of
decency drove him to defend Penelope.

"Whatever you may say of me, leave my sister out, if
you please. She had her faults, no doubt, but she is dead
now. Besides, we can't deny that she loved people and

124

sacrificed herself for them—look how she took care of Mr. Dombie—and that should be accounted to her for righteousness."

Sinkinda laughed again, and her laughter was musical but unpleasant. It frightened Timothy a good deal. "Keep a lady's name out of lewd conversation, eh? You and your fatuous chivalry! But tell me, my troubadour, what about Mr. Dombie—that poor man who should have been left to die? She brought him back from the grave, of course, she fought death for possession of him in a hand-to-hand encounter—and why? Because she needed a creature—her claque, her creation, if you like, a being she could command. You are too naïve to live."

These blasphemies shocked Timothy into silence. He stared at the hag, whose skin seemed to grow redder with excitement. She went on, "Why else would a woman want to bring back a man whose body was useless? Because such people make good victims; they have gone over to death, they have lost the will to live, and pride like your sister's can easily enter in and possess them. She called it devotion, of course, and it was love in a way—by stretching a point you might even call it passion—"

"Do you mean to imply—" began Timothy, as scarlet as the hag.

"Of course not! She remained technically chaste and he was—well, scarcely reanimated to that point, shall we say, to preserve your pseudo-Gothic front. Nothing so carnal as a love affair. But she used you both, nevertheless; she was the mother and the mistress—now don't

125

keep on denying it"—she held up her hand with author-
ity as Timothy started to speak; "innocence is really
very tiresome. Besides, you aren't being loyal to her;
you are just defending your own bad judgment, your
blindness, during all those years you lived under the
same roof."

Timothy tried not to remember a sound that rever-
berated from some deep place to which he had con-
signed it. It was the secret thud of Penelope's footsteps
as she would sometimes prowl about the house at night.
He would wake to the shuffling of bedroom slippers, he
would hear a faint tap-tap-tap on a door . . . "Did you
call, Mr. Dombie?" she would say. "Do you want anything?" "Have you enough blankets . . ." Then she
would fall back into the long silence; and after a while
he would, if he stayed awake, hear her going tiptoe upstairs again.

He did indeed feel compelled to defend his judgment, less against Sinkinda than against the suspicions
that unstrung him. "But Mr. Dombie *did* need the care
she gave him; she had to prepare all his food herself—
he had arteriosclerosis, you know, and couldn't touch
salt."

"Arteriosclerosis, my foot! Rigor mortis, that's what
ailed him. Of course she cooked his food herself; if they
eat salt, those renovated ruins, they know they're dead.
They break their bondage and go back to the freedom
and peace of the churchyard." She gave an affected little
titter.

Stung beyond enduring, Timothy jumped up. He

scarcely knew what he intended to do, it was only that the recklessness of anger and pity and wounded pride lifted him in spite of himself. But at his start Sinkinda sprang onto the rocker, balancing with her extraordinary air of being at ease in any element.

"Oho! Impatient to be out and riding, dear troubadour? Well, so am I"—and she made a sort of graceful dive toward him, touching the lamp as she passed so that it went out. Timothy dodged involuntarily; he felt foolish and furious—but what can you do but run—what use is valor with such a female? He ran. Once again his door opened into blind streets, anonymous as when he had walked them in the fog; but he was thankful enough that they were empty; he would have hated to be seen bolting, for bolting with him was the incredible being who had gained this dominance over his soul and whose ruthless doting he was unlikely ever to escape.

When Timothy woke next day it was noon. He was drunk with fatigue, but at least he wasn't dead, he thought—one good thing about hags, they didn't kill you, or not for a while. Groaning, he stretched his stiff limbs. The shadow of his horror still hung heavy about him and dissipated only by degrees as the motions of dressing, eating, and reading the paper restored him to his own shape. Fragments of his conversation with Sinkinda kept swimming into his mind in broken sequences; her accusations against Penelope gave him a queer stab of mingled horror and raw satisfaction. To be free from the bondage of that overshadowing goodness! But the issue was involved and sensational; he decided to forget it and did. Besides, Sinkinda, he thought (with a certain pleasure) was all woman; no doubt female rivalry entered into this fantastic interpretation of Penelope's character. The sharp hostility in her eyes when she talked about Penelope . . . the enormous black pupils . . . What was frightening about these eyes, they never returned your look, no recognition of another presence filled their emptiness. Come to think of it, they gleamed only with external light, when the quick turn of her head, the arching of her neck, brought her face to face with the fire or the lamp. Timothy gave a long startled sigh.

Toward dusk he sat on his front steps and watched the moon rise over the housetops while he assembled his arguments in case she should return that evening. He knew that, set against hers, his will would buckle like a stick of marsh sedge; still he wanted to state the case for Christian morality, for one didn't get over Christianity all at once, and he had by no means given up his inherited dogmas, definitive and comforting as they were.

That evening he did not even lock the door. He returned the washstand to its place under the splasher on the wall and made his room neat. In a little spurt of hospitality he put a bottle of port and two glasses on the table; it might not go well, but one could only try.

While he waited for his guest to arrive, he continued to talk to himself about Good and Evil. Precepts from the Scriptures poured into his mind; it was almost as if God had decided to take a hand in this battle. He alternately walked the floor in hope and threw himself down in despair, and he kept this up for a good part of the night.

When he heard a distant clock strike four and realized that the hag would not come, he felt distinctly flat. Now that he had some good arguments for her . . . It was unfair, just like a woman; the sex was congenitally weak in dialectic and in the sense of sportsmanship. Still, a good rest . . . He fell across the bed and sank into downy slumber.

The sound of church bells woke him. Sunday. . . . He stayed on the bed enjoying sheer laziness, the rare and blissful sense of having a long day ahead with nothing whatever to do. Belatedly he remembered his dinner engagement and sat up, swinging his bare feet to the floor with a thump. Anna Maria—he thought in dismay, the Iron Horse! His recent experiences had quite unfitted him to meet that large front of puffing energy, admirable as a steam engine. Even Will's robust good humor . . . He got up and wrote them a note asking them to excuse him today, he felt a little bilious.

When he had dispatched Pollo with the note, he bethought him of his neglected plants, and he put on some old clothes and went outdoors. The bare beds on either side the flagged walk had become two strips of fuzzy green, little vines had begun to reach greedy fingers up the brick wall. They had done surprisingly well, he reflected, mousing around, in spite of the shady lot; they poked out new leaves even in the places where dampness clung and the earth smelt sour.

The air of seclusion about his house which Timothy so cherished came from the livery stable building on one side and a tall dwelling on the other. At the back a transverse wall bounded the lot, along which he had planted kitchen herbs. Penelope would never allow chives or garlic in the old house, and he still felt guilt at offending against her canon of good taste. Nevertheless, he tended them carefully and made a pretty brick border to give them respectability. As he set to work now, debating with her the moral philosophy of eating garlic, he began to feel that someone was spying on him, and looking up he saw a disembodied head which had apparently come to rest on the wall above where he knelt. It was a female visitor, one very much alive and well fleshed. The sun shone on the hairpins in her brown hair, drawn into a seemly knot at the back of her neck; her light eyes, which were coolly taking his measure between their short black lashes, reflected in this leafy spot the green of nature with which she seemed allied. Timothy, who liked expressive eyes in a woman and long curling lashes, looked back at her in some distaste, not unmixed with nervousness.

"Good morning, Miss Farr," he said. "Won't you come in? You must be mighty uncomfortable up there, and certainly your appearance is odd—"

Broken bottles sunk in cement topped the wall to

discourage marauders, and the jagged points set off the
girl's face in a brightly wicked ruff.

She shook her head slowly and somehow her pointed
chin escaped the crystal blades. "You're sort of eerie-
looking yourself, Dr. Partridge, if we're going in for
personal remarks."

Timothy smoothed his short gray hair and brushed
the dirt off the knees of his trousers. "No—no; let's not
start in on personal remarks. I'm outgeneraled by your
eloquence in that field. But where do you keep yourself?
I never see you about town."

She craned her neck to get a better look at his plants
and Timothy was comforted to find it was attached to
a real pair of shoulders and surrounded by a conven-
tional pleated collar. She hoisted herself a little higher
and her hand appeared over the wall holding a straw
hat, which she laid on top of the broken glass as a
padding for her arm. "I've passed you once or twice
on the streets, but you were looking down as usual.
You don't waste much time on the world around you,
especially not on women. Or maybe it's just that I'm
not your style."

Timothy apologized hastily for having overlooked
her. "I've thought about you constantly since the day I
first saw you. You must have guessed that."

She smiled and did not deny it; after her fashion,
which Timothy found so irritating, she did not answer
him at all. Instead she surveyed the back of his house
curiously, her eyes dawdled over the plaster walls stained

with green, over the washtub, the back-yard rubble of brickbats and anonymous bits of rusty iron. Timothy took advantage of the moment to scrutinize her. Her nose was too long, he decided, for beauty; it was low and slender and her nostrils flared a little, like a trumpet. But before he could finish his scrutiny she turned back to him and asked, "What are you going to do with all these plants you've set out? Are you going back into pharmacy? I should think you'd be thankful not to be cooped up in that shop."

"No, I don't plan to open another shop. For one thing, very little of the equipment was saved from the fire— and even that is scattered."

She gave him a look full of humor and malice. "Well, you can loaf like a gentleman now. It must be nice to have plenty of money for a change."

Timothy thought quickly, if it's money she wants . . . Bribery was a novelty to him, another sweetmeat he could now indulge in; a device to try. He said, "Why don't you get down from that ridiculous position and come in? There are some questions I want to ask you—"

She laughed delightedly and showed for the first time her white teeth, set wide apart and slightly pointed. "Not today, thanks. I just ran by to see what you were up to, and now I've seen. My family will be putting bloodhounds on my trail if I don't get along home. Not that they bother their heads about me, except when they need me to get supper or something. You hoe your row, Dr. Partridge, and I'll hoe mine; you'll see me again, if you keep your eyes open." And she disappeared with surprising suddenness below the top of the wall.

He jerked open the back gate and stepped out into a narrow alley, down which he could see a figure skimming, her long skirts scalloping provocatively; she had already covered a considerable distance. But Timothy himself had learned to run, he had made the acquaintance of speed, and he went after her with all his new abandon. Before she reached the corner he caught up to her and seized her by the wrist.

"You're behaving like a spoiled brat," he panted. She gave him a furious look that threw him back a step, but he withstood its burning this time and kept his grip on her. "Now you're coming with me for a little talk. You have nothing to be afraid of—"

She let out a derisive mew at this idea and relaxed a little. Timothy pulled her along and found to his surprise that he was actually stronger than she; whatever he had expected, she was just an ordinary girl of flesh like his, and rather peaked, he thought, giving her a jerk. Suddenly he wondered what had come over him—he could imagine what Sister Penny would say about such carryings on. But her views, once so authoritative, now merely made a footnote in his mind; he continued to drag Miss Farr into his back yard.

He led her over to a tree whose gnarled roots, heaving out of the ground, formed a sort of rococo chair. Seating her in it, he planted himself opposite and looked directly at her.

133

"Why should you hate me?" he asked.

She grasped the root on either side of her fingers, which were long for one of her neat proportions. "What reason would I have to hate you?"

"That's what I want to know. After all, I gave you the ointment you wanted, though it was against my better judgment. And, by the way, how *is* your father's earache? Quite cured, I presume?"

She laughed again, throwing herself back against the trunk of the tree. "You have a budding sense of humor, after all. I didn't expect it."

Timothy, who considered he had a delightful sense of humor, looked affronted. She went on: "As a matter of fact, Father has another earache, and several new complaints besides. He's an old soak, so it's no wonder. But if that's what he wants, he can have it."

This disrespectful frankness shocked Timothy. "You are certainly heartless about your family."

"I have seven sisters and brothers—not counting three in the graveyard. You can't be expected to like nine people just because you live in the same house with them, can you? Some are less aggravating than others, of course. Still, you need lots of good servants to have time for brotherly love."

"I doubt if you'd have time for it—even if you had a palace staff. Brotherly love isn't your dish, I fancy. Tell me, did you get to the meeting that rainy night when you were in the shop?"

She looked away and said with the crisp intonation that made her replies sound slightly contemptuous,

"My group meets every month. I generally go." It might have been a sewing circle she was speaking of.

"Yes, on the full moon, I believe. They must be very lively meetings, with all the dancing, feasting, and love-making. And rather naughty, from what I've heard."

"You take life too much by hearsay. I can't imagine why I thought that evening you belonged . . . you were so stubborn about the solanum."

"I didn't know then—as you remarked before, I had a bad upbringing. I was taught that magic was all hokum."

"Thank goodness I wasn't Bible-raised," she said devoutly. "It just mixes people up about what's true and what isn't."

Timothy thought of Sinkinda and had no disposition to deny her and her witch-world a real existence.

Lucy was looking past the house at his front garden.

"If you have plenty of roots and herbs to sell, people will come for them with or without a shop. They'll come to the back gate, as they did before."

"Yes, they're beginning already; but it will take time to grow a supply. Nature can't be hurried, you know."

"Oh, but she can—that is, if you know the trick. But I have to go along." She gave him an obscure, glancing smile and put out her hand to be helped up.

Timothy pulled her to her feet.

"Well, Doctor, this visit has given me some ideas that may be useful to both of us. We'll talk about it some other time."

"Before you go I'd like to come to some agreement with you. If your circumstances are—er—cramped . . .

at home, I should say . . . I'm a man of liberal means now, as you just mentioned . . ." He blushed; he was really too new at it. Bribery was astonishingly difficult, especially with a lady.

She headed for the alley, tittering. "I'll stop by some other day."

As he caught up with her at the back gate, Timothy said again, "Do you hate me?"

She glanced at him, then away. "You flatter yourself. I don't either hate or like you. Has somebody got a grudge against you? It isn't easy to tell who your enemies are . . . why, people hate me I hardly even know. Take a still-hunt among your old customers, is my advice— for somebody your root-medicine disappointed. There must be hundreds! Pharmacists are natural targets for grudges."

"Oh," said Timothy. She went through the gate and down the lane without farewell.

Timothy had much to think of in the following days. Having been virtually shielded from women by natural timidity, poverty, and his sister, he was now faced with a feminine problem of the utmost complexity. He couldn't get over it. He thought of it by day as he weeded his garden and by night as he waited for the hag. Sinkinda, strangely enough, was far more real to him than Lucy; she had a stronger personality, he decided. Sinkinda—he rolled her name unctuously on his tongue. While he feared her to the marrow of his bones, she tempted him in a curious way, not of the flesh but of the imagination. He prepared a list of interesting topics to discuss with her, partly from a desire to raise himself from the low esteem in which she held him and partly in the hope of prolonging the pleasant side of her visits. The nights when she failed to appear were divided for him between chagrin and relief.

He began to wish he had a confidant, and thought a little of telling Will about this double conquest, of a sort, which he had made. But he could imagine Will, hearing such a tale. He would look at Timothy's tongue, feel his pulse, and tell him to take a course of calomel. The thought reminded Timothy that for the first time in his life he had omitted his spring dose, a ritual he followed with no less pious credulity than that of his remote pagan forefathers practicing their vegetation and fertility rites. How odd of him to have forgotten it! Then he did something that seemed to be in an equally odd way a substitute. He went back to the Palace Shaving Saloon and had his mustache taken off. When it had vanished in white foam he leaned forward and stared at himself in the barber-shop mirror. Why, I'm younger than I am!—was his first, his gratified thought—except for having gone gray. And except for an antique shape to his face—the clean jawline that seemed in its upward curve to drag the corners of his mouth with it in a marmoreal smile.

Getting ready to leave, he settled his tall collar, he hitched his coat up on his high shoulders and approved his rear view in the glass. Then bowing to the right and left he took his departure. But in the bright outdoors, his self-esteem collapsed. The sunlight played over his defenseless mouth like a sharper razor. He hurried along the sidewalk with his face to the wall, fearing people's eyes on his tender skin. This rigid and angular gait brought him close to the door of the butcher shop, and, seeing the sallow, plucked, and pimply fowls that hung there, he broke out in a cold sweat.

In the shelter of his own house, however, he gradually recovered his aplomb. He took the cunjer balls from the chimney and decided to give them to Pollo. He did not open them—no doubt they contained a lizard's foot, a black hen's feathers, the dried blood of a bat, and more such bane. Pollo was delighted with these as with all the hand-me-downs he received from Timothy, and went about the house with them tucked in the bosom of his shirt, where they made a horrid excrescence. After a while he said he had a toothache and, whether by associative magic or sheer ingenuity, developed a similar lump in his cheek. Timothy at length gave in and let him off. Pollo went delicately down the path cradling his jaw with one hand and his shirt-front with the other.

The following night Sinkinda came again. Timothy had fallen asleep in the rocker, so he did not know her means of entry on this occasion. He simply opened his eyes and found her sitting quite domestically in the armchair across the hearth.

"So you have graduated from Maum Rachel's magic, Doctor?"

"Well," said Timothy loyally, "Maum Rachel's magic might work, if circumstances—whom I don't care to name—were less contrary. You measure out the physic according to the disease, I suppose."

For the first time Sinkinda's smile was tinged with approval. "All magic has some potency; you are right not to despise the old woman. A small cat bone, a shred of hair, are sometimes the first steps to a larger design."

"I've been wanting to know—did you get hold of some of my hair as a first step?"

"Well, yes; there were other things I could have used, but this happened to be the easiest. I took a form which —doesn't matter," she looked at him severely, "and got it from the barber's sweepings. The raven black you had dyed it made it especially pleasing to work with."

"There—you're a romantic yourself," said Timothy triumphantly.

"Of course I am. You couldn't possibly imagine me as anything else."

"Do you mean that you are a figment of my imagination?"

"Partly so—human credulity is a great help in our profession—and partly not."

"Now that's just what I want to know," said Timothy eagerly, taking a pencil and an old envelope from his breast-pocket. "Admitting—purely for the sake of argument—that I am responsible in part, it does seem to me that you've taken things pretty much in your own hands. I never could have invented *you*. That's preposterous."

"So it is," she agreed complacently. "You see, there are parallels between magic and people's minds; your— indiscretions gave me the opening, I took the form your myth-making suggested. The rest is my own art." She took a little gold comb from her pocket and began coquettishly to smooth her hair. "But you ask too many questions. You're always trying to reduce mystery to a prescription and cork it up in a bottle. No one, I may say, has yet succeeded in that vaulting ambition." She deliberately changed the subject. "I see you've come further out of that thicket you've been hiding in."

"Oh, that . . ." Timothy spoke offhand, but he rubbed his upper lip self-consciously. "I suppose it's odd to go clean-shaven; people think I look very old-timy." He glanced hopefully at her for a disclaimer.

Sinkinda nodded, and her hollow cheeks, flushed like the inside of a shell, quivered slightly. "'Old-timy' is an understatement. A throwback—that's what you look like. And are. You could have been taken down off the portal of a fourteenth-century cathedral and set to walking about. Well, that elongation of the figure is at least a distinguished trait—" She put her head back and surveyed him from between half-closed lids.

Timothy blushed with gratification and ran to pour out the port. She refused, however, the glass he offered. "The trouble with living high is that it spoils you. You get used to the best. Frankly, I haven't the stomach for human provender. It's ill-seasoned stuff."

"Too much red pepper, perhaps?" said Timothy hazardously.

The hag's skin began to glow alarmingly as if he had blown on her with a pair of bellows. "You're a blundering kind of fellow; and all that dabbling in books has

140

only fuddled your wits. Hags of the cruder sort slip their skins and leave them behind doors, but my tribe knows better ways to ride the air. We have secret ointments that take off only the outer layers of skin—"

"Oh. Like cantharides, or even sunburn—"

Sinkinda ignored this pharmaceutical analysis. "These agents make the body more sensitive to the buoyant powers naturally in the air. The ordinary human hide is too thick for such fine responses. As to red pepper, I hate the stuff just the same, and tomorrow by fowl-crow you will sweep it all up. And don't waste any more of it about these premises."

"Yes, ma'am," said Timothy, regretting that he had ever mentioned this irritant. He tried hard to remember his list of suitable topics but they eluded him. Well, Good and Evil always remained, and he began to question her earnestly about them. She laughed, this time with genuine amusement in her voice. "There you go again. Man, the moralist—what a figure of fun! You ought to be in a Punch and Judy show."

"But I love to argue about morals. What subject is more absorbing! Actually, everybody has an itch to understand them, to find out why Evil plagues us and what we ought to be doing about it."

"Satan is everywhere," said the hag sedately. "Not much you can do about that."

"Everywhere" was a territory Timothy was used to ascribing to God. He thought hard for a while. "There's something in what you say. Temptation swarms around us; and there's a natural depravity in inanimate things that's quite shocking, when you think of it. It's always the jar of ointment that's troublesome or expensive to mix that falls in the sink and smashes. And Sister's spool of thread was forever rolling under the china press instead of under some movable article of furniture."

"And you always had to go down on all fours to get it. Yes, that would have given her pleasure."

"But *she* didn't roll it under the china press; come, now, be reasonable."

"Perhaps not; but she was always very gracious, wasn't she, seeing you down on all fours?"

"You are certainly bitter about my sister." Timothy gulped his port. "And you're only partly right. She did, I suppose, enjoy her power over Mr. Dombie, but that she had a guilty passion for him I will not believe."

Sinkinda drew her shapely legs up and clasped her hands around them. She laid her head against the high tufted back of the chair, whose carved and pointed frame had rather the look of a dark throne. "I suppose you never asked yourself why she raised such an outcry about your going away?"

This disinterring of his last quarrel with Penelope threw Timothy into a violent and painful agitation. He looked down at his feet, trying to dodge the question shining from the demi-lunes of the hag's eyes.

In the end Sinkinda answered the question herself. "She couldn't have lived there with Mr. Dombie if you had left. A common dwelling is as useful to the relationship of owner and slave as to what you call a guilty passion."

142

Timothy tried to suppress a groan, but the sound would not be swallowed. Sinkinda pressed her advantage. "Penelope was always making a virtue into a vice by carrying it to extremes. Her excessive pity for Mr. Dombie, for her pensioners, for all her objects of charity, was really sentimentality, a mold, because at bottom it was self-pity. She had an affinity with the weak.

"The truth is, the aftermath of a war makes an invigorating climate for Satan, especially in the defeated territory. Just imagine, for one thing, the keening of all those leftover women after their lost mates—what a head of steam for some imaginative leader to use! Penelope turned to and got herself up a man of sorts; but without professional help, which she was too stubborn to ask, she did a clumsy job. Still, crude as he was, he made her feel essential."

"Now, wait," said Timothy, with dogged reasonableness. "You must remember this: Sister grew up in prosperity, she knew what it was like to have pretty dresses and good food, yet after the War she denied herself for people, she gave up the material things—which, if you are right about her, she must have wanted—in order to help them."

Sinkinda gave a little cluck of affected astonishment. "Can you imagine a handsome woman like Penelope going round in those mildewed-looking clothes? You cannot. She appeared to be without vanity, but, mark me, she was eaten up with vanity. She wore poverty like a bustle, she turned self-denial wrong side out and made it into a new coat. Remember how eloquent she used to get about the richness and materialism of the North? One of her best subjects—because she really loathed her own poverty. Sour grapes easily turn to vinegar in the veins."

Sinkinda's words were having a curious effect on Timothy . . . he felt a loosening at his throat, like taking off his high tight collar when he came home from church on Sundays. His head and limbs felt light; he gulped another glass of port.

"I must say, you've made it all very confusing—this business of good and bad," he said.

"Has it ever occurred to you that they might be the same thing—or at least complementary?"

"They are not in the least the same thing. You are a wicked and cynical woman. Although a very charming one," he added, from natural politeness and fear of reprisal.

Sinkinda clucked again. "I'm a hag, and my means of locomotion give me more perspective than you get, tied to the ground. Tell me, do you believe that God is the maker of heaven and earth and of all that is under the earth?"

"Of course. That's axiomatic."

"Well, then—the Creator must have made Evil too. You must believe that Satan is His handiwork, which you shouldn't despise."

"Oh, God!" cried Timothy in vexation, "I wish I knew! I've cudgeled my brain black and blue over that question."

"Centuries of cudgeling have gone on over that ques-

144

tion, in monasteries, libraries, pulpits, and wilderness retreats. How theologians love to trip themselves up over something quite simple! The truth is that Good and Evil are inseparable; when God came into existence, Satan sprang like His shadow from the same spot and equally created God. Good . . . Evil; light . . . shadow; pleasure . . . pain—none of these could exist without its opposite."

Timothy's stomach sank. Perhaps she's right, he thought, perhaps morality is just an alternation and can never be fixed in a code. He pulled his upper lip so long over this that Sinkinda said sharply, "The Heaven you dream of is an absurdity. Perfection would be nothingness without Evil to point it up. The trouble with you is the Christian myth surrounded you at birth like a caul from which you've never emerged."

Timothy was an obstinate man and he had one more argument. "But if Good can't exist without Evil, then bad people serve God's purpose just as well as good people."

Sinkinda gave him a honeyed smile. "And have a lot more fun. Generations of men live and die without discovering that simple truth."

"Let's go!" exclaimed Timothy, starting up. He was suddenly sick of morals; the open road lured him from a controversy of which he was not getting the better.

A powerful contralto crying "Buyeyster!" sounded down the block, and Timothy took a pan and went out. The morning sun beamed on his face; his whole being sopped it up as he leaned on the front gate. It's as good as Brown's Iron Bitters, he thought, strengthens the nerves, purifies the blood, invigorates the constitution. And doesn't taste bad. While he waited for the oyster-woman, the natural world came up in all its clarity and crowded round him. He watched a chameleon on the gatepost sunning its brilliant green back. It turned its bulging eyes on him warily; the skin of its neck, wrinkling in tiny folds, made it look timeless, the descendant of dragons. The harsh angle of leg and thigh, the little spraddled hands, the pointed reptilian head, were fierce and endearing. As he stood relishing this little fantasy of nature's, the lizard threw back its head, jerked it as if it were about to neigh, but instead of a sound it puffed out its blanket of innocent petal-pink from its throat and drew it in again.

"Eh-eh! De mo' feller leetle de mo' he have to strut some." A round brown face appeared on the other side of the gate.

"That's so, Mamie," said Timothy, enchanted with both of them. "I feel like strutting a little myself." He handed her his pan, which she filled from the cedar pail. Today she gave him an extra ladleful.

Encouraged by this sign of favor, he began to ask questions. "What do you think about Good and Evil?"

The oysterwoman had certain curious identities with her wares. "No, sir," she said with finality, and, dropping the dipper into her bucket, prepared to move.

"Hold on a minute. Do you know Mr. Farr's youngest daughter, Miss Lucy?"

146

"No, sir."

Whether it was caution or conspiracy, the Negroes of the town would give him nothing. He and Mamie scanned each other closely and deliberated for a moment.

From the corner of his eye Timothy saw a slight movement above his head and backed off a little. On the gatepost crouched the brindled cat, watching the lizard, which still basked just below. The cat's pale eyes with their narrow vertical slits were fixed in menace; the tip of her tail waved. Slowly she raised and extended one hooked paw.

"Scat!" Timothy shouted in the cat's face. With a furious yellow glance she dropped from the wall and streaked across the garden. The lizard, too, sprang off the post and scuttled among the leaves and twigs. Through the powerful force of its fear, its color changed before Timothy's eyes to a drab greenish-brown as it lost itself among the weeds.

"That damned cat—she'd better leave my lizards alone. I like having lizards around," he explained; "they keep down the mosquitoes and the pests that eat my plants."

Lizards, the oysterwoman agreed, were good for all sorts of things, but bad too if the wrong set of people got hold of them. Some people could slip in at night and put one inside your head if they wanted to harm you. Then you woke up choking and might die of shortness of breath, or your blood might turn to clabber. Sperrits were mischee-vous this time of year; everybody better be careful. She grasped the handles of her barrow,

147

and with a great shout of "Buyeyster!" she trundled along the pavement.

Timothy couldn't make out whether a warning coiled in these generalities or not. Mamie, he had decided, did not "belong." She merely acknowledged the baffling tactics of both God and the Devil and kept out of the controversy as far as possible. Yet he recognized in her some quality sturdy and profound that brought him reassurance. Like a convert who finds another believer, he took comfort that she shared his heterodoxy.

That afternoon he had another visit from Lucy. This time she came boldly in at the front gate, listing under the weight of the large basket on her arm.

"Good evening," cried Timothy, hurrying to welcome her. But when they met in the path she stopped short, and gave him a mischievous glance. "You look like the Devil!"

As always her bold manners both shocked him and aroused a sneaking admiration. He covered his shorn upper lip with his hand and said self-consciously, "Is that an aspersion or a compliment?"

"Whichever you like. The shape of your face is clear, now. That's all."

Clearly stamped, he gathered, with a paternity not of the Partridges. Was he a changeling in the cradle, then? But he fastidiously rejected the taint of bastardy; he preferred to think his great misdeeds had earned him this distinction, or even his little misdeeds—his first dabblings in magic, his unchristian attitude to Mr. Dombie . . .

She had come to help him with his garden, Lucy was saying, since it was plain that, left alone, he'd never make anything of it.

Timothy took the basket. "You shouldn't be carrying this—it weighs a ton."

"Oh, I'm strong," she assured him. "Small but wiry." She took off her hooded cape; her head, her neck, and her little high bosom emerged from its folds, and Timothy said, "Small but personable, let us say."

Her shrug was half-challenging. She began to unpack the basket, which yielded surprises. A bag of fertilizer, a bottle, and at the bottom two of the blue English-ware jars from Timothy's shop. "Where did you get them?" he cried with vexation and delight.

"I saved them from the fire. And several others—I'll bring them next time. You can use them when the plants are ready to be ground up. I scorched my fringed shawl to get them out."

Timothy could well imagine her dashing into the burning house to bring out some trifle she wanted. "You're a silly girl, and a bad one, I'm afraid. You stole my jar of frogs and newts, too."

"I stole nothing," she said sourly. "I paid you extra for them—fifteen cents extra. Remember? That's a lot for dried frogs. I needed them for something special. And I'm returning the blue jars now."

They fell to work on the plants, Lucy weeding while Timothy fed them. He tested the dark mixture in the bag with nose and thumb and decided it was better not to ask what composed it. It smelt evil enough to pro-

149

duce a Malay jungle in his meager yard. While their hands flew in these congenial tasks, they talked with devout absorption of the properties of plants and the uses, scientific or otherwise, to which they could be put. Lucy told him about a garden in her neighborhood that had some rare shrubs in it; she had the habit of snipping off a few twigs when she went by—very few, not enough to hurt anybody. "And do you know"—she sat back on her heels and held her trowel pointed outward, ready to plunge it in some adversary's heart—"a man ran out one day and drove me away with a broomstick? Told me to keep my evil eye off his place!"

"What did you do?"

"Oh, I put the triple curse on him—it was all I could do for the moment. I cursed the whole lot—from the head of the house to the nannygoat in the back yard! 'Evil eye, is it?' I said. 'Very good—I'll put it on you.'"

Timothy, the moralist, was revolted by this amorality, but Timothy, the postulant of Evil, found it as stimulating as a dose of strychnine.

Darkness drove them at last from their congenial occupation. Lucy hated to stop, she could see perfectly well, she said, but Timothy insisted on gathering up the tools. "Well, I'll come back and finish the work some other time. Perhaps I'll tell you now about my idea. I think we should go into partnership. You have the ground, I have the knack of growing things. We could make money."

"Look here, you can't keep coming to my house like this. People will gossip."

"Gossip?" The word blew from her lips like a soap bubble and floated harmlessly across the garden. "I don't think that will bother us. Luckily you moved into a bad neighborhood; nobody here has a good name to lose."

"All the same," he said, leary of the scheme, "it would be better perhaps if I went to your house. If you should ever run into my cousin, Anna Maria Golightly, the fat would be in the fire."

Lucy glowered. "I'd love to meet Mrs. Golightly here."

"Oh, do you know her? What have you got against her? They're a nice wholesome pair, the Golightlys—"

"They are that. Anna Maria is so wholesome she makes me feel sick. And the fatuous way they go on about those nasty dogs of theirs—" Timothy could almost see her fur rising.

Her opinion of the Golightlys, he found with a pang, precipitated the change that was taking place toward them in his own feelings. As he sat torn between loyalty and candor, she interrupted: "By the way—here's a bottle of hair tonic for you. You look kind of funny, you know, with those short bristles. This is a special mixture; it'll bring results, I promise you."

Timothy took the bottle and mumbled his thanks. She threw her hooded cape around her with an unconscious grace that pounced on him from its folds and wiped out his doubts; in the falling dusk the long pure lines gave her the severe sweetness of a primitive madonna—a freakish resemblance, he had to add. He

151

escorted her as far as the car line, but she refused curtly to allow him to see her home.

Her enthusiasm for his plants so beguiled Timothy that he thought he could see them growing. She came in quite often, and, as she had predicted, his neighbors proved difficult to scandalize. No one seemed to notice them as they dug, snipped, and compared notes on the old fields and moist places outside the city where rare plants could be found; Lucy, too, loved the fungi, the ferns and mosses that grew in dripping hollows, the reedy grasses in the woods-pools, a taste that went with her white skin under which the delicate blue veins ran like the tracing of a leaf. They planned expeditions to the country to collect herbs.

Between his day and his night activities, Timothy lived through the spring in a state of high inebriation. As the weather warmed he gave up having a fire, and Sinkinda took to coming by the shorter route of his own chimney. He looked forward eagerly to his talks with her; their elevated moral plane gave him great satisfaction. The rides were still a nightmare, an experience of tingling fear and humiliation, but after a while he began to feel a thread of perverse pleasure even in these, as victims are said to come to love their torturers. Moreover, his muscles and heart gradually adjusted themselves to this exercise. Each time he woke up less tired the following day. You can get used to anything, he reflected complacently.

Sinkinda for her part seemed to ride him more

lightly all the time. "You are really an accomplished equestrienne," he told her one evening. She crowed derisively, but he had an idea that his old-fashioned compliment pleased her. In a strange way he began to find her beautiful; her fluid limbs, built for riding on air, her sultry eyes and brow, even the curious sanguine of her skin from which the purposeful blood seemed ready to burst with its own verve—all her subtle violence of mind and body held him in a wondering thralldom.

One evening as Timothy and Lucy were absorbed in their stint on the flower beds he noticed that the dark came very suddenly, and looking up he saw a tall black cloud standing djinnlike above his wall. Immediately it began to cast its swollen drops down on them. They snatched up their tools and ran for shelter; the storm lashed at them from behind and beat on the closed door. The pounding of the tropical downpour on the roof and shutters brought Timothy a heady delight, for with Lucy in the house he felt safe from menace. Bursting with hospitality, he got out some cold victuals and a bottle of wine, and they had a gay supper to the wild fiddling outdoors like the strains of a demoniac band hidden in the shrubbery.

Timothy's study, where they set their table, had lost its bare look and begun to acquire the congenial clutter of his old home. His blue jars shone on the shelves; he had raked the secondhand shops for old books, which he seldom had time to read but which gave the study an air he fondly imagined to be Faustian. He had even acquired a pair of carboys and mixed a purple liquid for them even more alchemical than the green and amber tinctures in his shop windows.

Their somber gleam took Timothy's mind back to the shop and his first sight of Lucy, blown into his life from a rainy world like this one. As then, the wildness pelting from above communicated itself to her, and through her to him. They had come a long and devious way (the more he considered it) from the shop to this evening alone in his private apartment; their seclusion flicked his imagination, or that part of it which begins in the channels of the blood.

He wanted to take her hand, but, in spite of a new daring in his heart, he was at a loss how to make the first move with a creature so ambiguous.

The rain enclosed them in a sort of dream where everything turned topsy-turvy. To add to Timothy's confusion, words, which he had always looked on as solids, had changed their content—they weren't at all what they used to be. Righteousness had become a dreary virtue; piety—how sniveling it sounded; and virtue itself—how undesirable. As to love, he hadn't the glimmer of an idea what thing it meant.

Lucy, of course, made no effort to talk, and nowadays he found their silences not awkward but more communicative than speech. He went and stood beside her chair. After a time he said, "Love is the most changeable of words . . . like a great net of fish. I loved my sister, you know—was it good or evil? It used to seem right—"

154

"But you carefully fixed things so the house would burn up and rid you of her."

"So I did. I had to do it. I can see her now—a fine, upstanding woman, with fine strong bones. And her will was a bone. Even her blue eyes were calcareous. Nothing but fire would destroy her."

"I don't see why you didn't do it long ago."

Speaking thus of his act in the most natural manner in the world, Timothy stood taller. What guilt he felt was for having been a sedulous brother all those years.

Lucy relapsed into silence, and again it was Timothy who broke it. "I don't even wonder that you know all this about me. But I also know about you. You are Sinkinda somehow; I can't understand by what sort of saturation."

"I'm changeable too; I've learned how to go from our world to the other—and back. Let's let it go at that. But you've done some changing yourself."

There was challenge even in the way she sat, her feet on the rungs of the chair, and turned her eyes on him with some of their old intensity. He shivered—and felt suddenly warm again. Her image wavered before his eyes, perhaps because he had taken off his spectacles and slipped them into his pocket, but even without them he was fully aware of the real girl under her inappropriate flounces and of her appeal to something that was explicitly human and physical.

She got up restlessly and said, "It has stopped raining." It was true; there was a sharp cessation of all noise, as if everyone living had been drowned.

Lucy went toward the door and Timothy followed her, carrying the lamp. Their shadows leapt before them. In the hall they stood and looked at each other, their faces full of brilliance and darkness across the fluted chimney. They stood thus a long time, then Lucy put her hand around the top of the chimney and blew the light out. Timothy set the lamp on the hall table, and as he bent down, he felt her arms about his neck. A thrill of purely reflex fear shook him; but it passed as he found them round and real, her fingers warm and desiring. He turned and kissed her in the circle they made, a magic circle he could not break nor wanted to.

After that Lucy came at night, not Sinkinda. Timothy never knew when she would appear; she forbade him to call at her house or even to write—her sisters would pry into the letters. So he had to wait upon her caprice, to sit through long evenings listening for the little stirs and scratches in the yard that heralded her approach. These vigils anguished him as sharply as his waits for Sinkinda had, with the difference that his fear now was that his visitor would not come.

In Lucy, Sinkinda's wildness was mixed with qualities endearingly human—her nipping sense of fun, her little jealousies, her love of contention for its own sake —each time she left him she tied on her shawl with a brisk air of going forth to a potential conflict. Their conversation ran to distinctly less elevated topics, but on the whole he was satisfied with the exchange.

Timothy worked the garden mostly by himself now,

digging furiously to get through the hours until Lucy should arrive. But the plants flourished without her ministrations; perhaps her thumb was so potently green that it had been enough for her merely to give them a start, or perhaps it was the potently smelling fertilizer that accounted for their prodigal growth.

His hair also grew astonishingly; under his faithful applications of the tonic it sprouted white and vigorous from his scalp. This gave rise to a fable in the town that his hair had turned white in a single night from the shock of the fire—but when, Timothy, reflected, had fable ever let itself be corrupted by fact? And he encouraged the story in small ways as he went about his business. The curve of his lips grew more sardonic; it would have delighted his Gothic soul if he could have let it be known that he was the lover of a hag. Only that vestigial virtue, a gentleman's honor, sealed his lips.

He took a sudden interest in dress and selected for himself a handsome black suit with a three-button coat. His figure, alas, still resembled a bed-slat; night-traveling did nothing to put flesh on one's bones. A new oxblood waistcoat with a gold watch chain across it lent him, he thought, studying himself in his looking glass, a touch of desirable corpulence. He had mislaid his watch some time back; having shed people, he had rid himself of the necessity for petty divisions of time, but charms on watch chains were popular this season, an attractive and practical fashion. His glasses spent more time on the bureau and less on his nose; he had never really needed them to see the world, he found; only to keep from being seen. He still had a hankering for raven hair, but Lucy forbade him to resort to dye. "You'll do very well as you are, Timothy; with your young face and that white mop, you are something to make people turn around and stare. The combination is kind of stylish and kind of perverse. I like you that way."

If this were true, Timothy was intoxicated with perversity—another changeling word. And whatever Lucy liked in him was right and desirable. That she should condescend to his companionship filled him with wonder, as indeed did everything about her. Holding her on his knee in the big armchair in his room, he questioned her closely about her life.

"Tell me, dearest, how did you come to take up this —er—career?"

"Hagging? Oh, some people are just bad. I was born mean, I suppose."

"You certainly aren't one to mince matters. But when did you actually go over to the Adversary?"

Wriggling a little—she had a cat's aptitude for making the lumps and hollows of a lap serve her comfort— she let her head fall back on his shoulder. Her charming profile close to his cheek was turned up to the ceiling in a rare moment of relaxation and intimacy. "It came about naturally. I hate my life, and why shouldn't I? That crowded pigsty of a house! So I took to going out at night by myself . . . night is lovely, you don't have to look at a lot of stupid faces . . . and people held it against me that I wasn't afraid of the dark the way they are. Then, my disposition *is* kind of surly—oh, I don't know,

158

maybe it's just because my eyebrows are black, it could be as easy as that—anyway, they began to say I had the evil eye; they left me to myself, and even my sisters banded together against me. Well, old tales often come true that way: they said I had an evil eye, so I had one. You can well imagine that for once I was obliging."

"But how," Timothy persisted, "did you make a start? How did you learn the tricks?"

She seemed loath to go into particulars. "If you hate a place enough, and you are cooped up there, you escape into another plane. Now, you were tied down too, and took a pretty sweeping way of getting clear—" She nipped his cheek with her little white fangs.

Lucy managed to have her own kind of fun with hagging, Timothy learned. She kept Mrs. Sawyer awake all one night by snipping her nose with a pair of pincers; she tied people's hair in knots, and upset buckets of paint on the show-offs who walked under ladders. Timothy laughed till he cried at her account of having ridden Mr. Sylvester Sheedy, the prominent politician; that was a treat! she said—he had more gaits than a circus horse, but she had let him off finally because he made monkeys of so many smart people, and now she just doubled him up with cramps every once in a while.

"And by the way, what on earth made you pick me, a harmless pharmacist plying his trade?"

"Oh, I didn't like that solemn scientific manner of yours when I came into the shop. I could tell you were ripe for something of this sort; and when I got to the

159

fire and found you weren't in it I knew right away what had happened. Then that bad conscience of yours made you come after me and give yourself away."

Timothy rubbed his forehead thoughtfully as if to test the offending member presumably located within.

The first clear day Timothy hired a horse and buggy from the livery stable, and they drove across the New Bridge into the country. Lucy had dressed up for him in her best dove-wing silk, and the silent compliment, the only kind she ever paid him, set his blood singing. The dress, tightly buttoned from the turnover collar to the hem, gave her small provocative person a Sunday-school artlessness which tickled his palate immensely. Her round hat with a feather circling its upturned brim was new and the occasion of a good deal of preening.

Having found a woody copse on the river's edge, they set out with basket and trowel to collect plants. Lucy seemed as verdantly innocent and fresh as the day; the bright painted weather on wood and river had blunted the grieving thorns she went armed with. " 'Gentle as falcon or hawk of the tower,' " Timothy quoted fondly; and for once she did not ridicule his sentiment. On a congenial impulse they unbuttoned their shoes and kicked them off to feel the fuzzy green shag of the earth with the soles of their feet. Nature was in a bounteous mood. The herbs piled up in the basket, the lure of the chase carried them through bogs, under-brush, and briars after spotted wintergreen and moth mullein, ginseng, and the lowly Jimson weed—"The stramonium extracted from Jimson weed has had re-

160

markable results in curing mania," Timothy instructed her lovingly.

Lucy suggested that by a slight alteration it could be turned to more amusing uses.

"I know," Timothy said, not to be outdone; "magicians have sometimes used the seeds to induce hallucinations. It's one of the fascinating ambiguities of the plant world."

"How tiresome education makes people," said Lucy yawning. The yawn was amiable and intimate, however.

Timothy looked at her abashed. He was beginning to discover that Lucy had been given little schooling, and indeed he could not imagine what a schoolmistress would do with such a pupil. She never, he noticed, wrote anything down—a habit repugnant to his accurate pharmacist's mind; sometimes he wondered if she could write. . . . "I remember things without putting them down," was her only answer to his tactful inquiries.

He thought of Penelope and her orphanage. "Education may make people tiresome sometimes; still, it widens their horizons and enriches their lives, you have to admit."

"Oh, I don't know. You learn things for yourself— or else you don't; and in that case I doubt if books can help you."

The very novelty of the idea bowled him over. His beloved books . . . so many sere leaves? So many cobwebs to ensnare the brain?

They talked then of their herbs and what they could

do with them, how to compound and how to dispose of them. "We'll write to the mountains for some others," Lucy said. "I have an acquaintance there, a witch doctor, who will send us samples from his part of the country. We must build up a good supply so we won't have to depend on the smelly apothecaries—forgive me, darling, you've graduated from that profession." She kissed both his cheeks consolingly. "It was only the bad drought last fall, you know, that got me into your clutches . . . or you into mine."

Timothy was too beglamoured with her clutches to take offense at any word of hers. He brought a carriage rug and a hamper from the buggy and spread their lunch by the water. When they had restored themselves with cold capon and claret, they walked up and down under the trees talking about everything imaginable, and with earth, heaven, and hell for their fields of interest they could scarcely pause to draw breath.

One sorrow to him, however, was that Lucy's attention wandered when he tried to discuss morals with her. It seemed to him that, as Lucy, she thought differently from Sinkinda—or, perhaps, thought less; in the process of translation Sinkinda was abstracted to the more purely spiritual and intellectual element. Under his prodding, Lucy lazily produced a somewhat different view of the theory that so concerned him. "If you want my opinion," she said, chewing a blade of grass, "it's that through the ages people have called the opposition the Devil. They are always laying the new idea to Satan —whatever jolts their notions of good. He's none too pleased about this, I'm sure—lots of new ideas are half-baked. But he's hardened to being misunderstood."

"But according to that theory, life is sheer confusion. There's no Good or Evil that you can hold on to." Timothy ruffled his brow in distress. "Don't you even desire a moral order?"

"I think it's moonshine; you're just being frivolous."

His pained face sent her rolling over in shrieks of laughter; she began to tease him, she tweaked his nose, she pulled off his red waistcoat and hid it, she sailed his new straw hat over the bluff into the river. Then she slipped out of her long hot dress and ran about the woods in her chemise. Timothy chased after her, torn between delight and jealousy lest some other eye than his should see her thus.

Seeing her thus himself gave him the idea of spending the night there in the woods. Lucy agreed instantly; they had brought much more food than they could eat, so they had the leftovers for supper. Their fund of conversation seemed to burgeon rather than fade. Timothy drew on the list of suitable topics that he had prepared for Sinkinda, while Lucy produced a string of diverting stories—about a neighbor of hers who had died of spontaneous combustion and how at the autopsy they had found a pound and a half of snuff in her head; about the Hunter's Chapel murder, and the beautiful young woman who had shot down a prominent citizen of the Up-Country and left him in his blood on the church floor; about—and this was Timothy's favorite—the Devil's driving up in his gig to call on the L——s, who welcomed and wined the distinguished stranger and were quite put out to have him run off at cockcrow and jump clean across the Congaree River.

When other topics failed they talked interminably about themselves and their growing attachment to each other. Since even the most exotic love affair is not spared the curse of earthly imperfection, the sandflies and mosquitoes settled down on them with the darkness; they rubbed themselves with pennyroyal and built a smudge fire of moss, which at least discouraged their tormentors. They lay cosily on the carriage rug watching the dull embers and the pale flower of the smoke as it opened, swayed, drooped against the blue midnight. The thickets rustled with stalkers; it seemed to Timothy that in striking the match he had shattered Time, that this fire was one with the campfires of a thousand years which had held off the sleepless animal hunger; he and Lucy lost a personal identity in the long tale of man's loving and mating; even his rapt interest in the supernatural encounter, the unseen made flesh, was as old as curiosity and fear.

They stirred and sought words for the miracle. *You are mine now . . . I never felt this way before.* The vain and foolish vows—*Love me and keep me*—constantly made and tragically forsworn. *Is it real? Is it I? Is it you? It's like falling through a dream.* The old sayings became rich with great substance; the variable word suddenly stood solid.

"The miraculous thing is that miracles do happen."

"The trouble is to keep them. They slip through your

fingers," Lucy murmured. But Timothy didn't believe this, for he had fed on honeydew and drunk the milk of paradise.

All this time he had not heard from the Golightlys except a letter from Anna Maria asking why he didn't come to Sunday dinner, a letter he didn't answer. At length Will's buggy stopped at his door, and Will himself came stamping up the brick walk. "Hullo, there!" he cried on catching sight of Timothy, then halted in an amazement he could not conceal. With unusual tact, however, he choked back his comments on Timothy's appearance. "Where've you been hiding yourself? I hear you've turned hermit since I been away." He had taken a vacation, a fishing trip—"You should 'a' been along, Tim—it would 'a' stirred up your sluggish liver."

His fish stories spared Timothy for some time the awkwardness of answering his questions. Eventually, however, he narrowed his circumambient talk and focused on his cousin. "What you gonna do with all that stuff you got planted out there? Open a new pharmacy? If you won't hump yourself and get out of here, that's as good a way to invest your money as any."

"No," said Timothy, looking vague. "I don't want to run a pharmacy all my life. It's too confining. The world is too full of interesting things to see and do."

Will's thatchy eyebrows rose half an inch in his full-blooded face. "Well, this is a conversion! Just what I been trying to tell you all these years. You ought to get out into the country. The hunting season's over, of course; but why don't you try riding? That'll tone up your muscles like nothing else."

Timothy said he had tried riding and it had toned up his muscles, but on the whole he considered it a crude sport. "Regarding it from the viewpoint of the horse, I mean."

Will stared at him in amazement and some anxiety. "Well, come on and go devilfishing with me next month at Port Royal, Tim. There's a sport fit for the gods! There's no sensation in the world, lemme tell you, like being dragged along hell-for-leather by one of those monsters!"

Timothy stifled a shiver and said politely, "No, thanks, old man."

"Come," Will insisted, "you can't sit down on your hunkers all your life; are you just living on your capital? It won't hold out long at that rate, you know."

Timothy admitted he hadn't even looked at his bank-book for quite a while. "I don't take any interest in accounts, these days."

"Hell and death! You ought to do something with your capital."

Timothy just stared. He really couldn't explain that "ought" and "should" had lost their content for him; they looked brown and frail as locust shells, he had thrown his out with the trash.

"See here, maybe you'd like to invest it in a promising little venture—I could put you on to a good thing I'm taking a flier in myself. It might be kind of hard for you to go back into the drug business; I've had to send all my patients to Dr. Lockwood while you were dawdling round, and you'd have to start from scratch, especially as Lockwood runs a good, up-to-date pharmacy."

Timothy did not feel like answering, so he didn't. Instead he occupied his mind with his cousin, whose person, as he stood there—grizzled, flat-footed, no nonsense or woolgathering about him—seemed quite fantastic. At all events he no longer desired Will's reality, uncertain as his own might be.

The rudeness of his silence flicked Will's temper. "Good God, Tim! You *got* to pull yourself together! There's no excuse for just going to the dogs like this!"

What was it that going to the dogs used to mean? Timothy wondered. Not this, not the heady discovery of an unknown world in which all his five senses seemed to waken at once to a delight in whatever was wry, nonsensical, other—that is, other than it appeared. Yet— he looked down at his bare feet, at his shirt open on his chest, he remembered the inexplicable bush of white hair above his face, now brown as snuff from working out of doors, and he thought he saw Will's point of view.

This second silence disturbed Will even more. He shifted his big feet and looked about the place. At length he said, "Well, I better be on the jump—Anna Maria will pick me clean if I'm late for dinner again."

Timothy accompanied him to the gate and so far recovered himself as to ask after the family. They were all pretty well, Will said. Anna Maria was having a spell of the cramps, but he couldn't find anything the matter with her. Sometimes he suspected she was just putting on.

"The little hussy!" Timothy muttered with a grin he couldn't suppress.

"How's that?" Will's eyes started in his hairy incredulous face.

"Oh . . . not Anna Maria! Great God, no, I didn't mean *her!* I was thinking of somebody quite different. Excuse me, old man—"

At the gate they parted sadly, having nothing to say to each other.

Timothy lived on excitements, however, that left little room in his mind for regrets. There were other picnics with Lucy, and the care of their collection of herbs, which had now spread all over the back yard as well as the front. She could scarcely wait to transmute these vegetable riches into minerals; like Will, she had a mundane interest in bank accounts. "You're a horrid little materialist," said Timothy stroking her hair. "Money doesn't bring happiness, really."

"Huh—does poverty bring it? Not that I ever saw. Who hatched up the silly idea that poverty refines character? Well, I've forgotten him, and he ought to be in limbo. Being poor soured my nature a long time ago."

The amazing results of the hair tonic gave them an idea. Lucy divulged its formula to Timothy, who set about concocting and bottling it; he had a neat label printed—"Partridge's Hirsutus: Makes Hair Grow on a Rock." This persuasive legend or the miraculous

168

properties of the tonic made it an immediate success. The back-door customers multiplied, even well-placed persons sent their servants for a bottle or two of this wonderful restorative. A mild typhoid epidemic, followed by an epidemic of shaved heads, greatly increased their trade. Timothy couldn't help urging the victims to boil their cistern water in future with snakeroot, advice which Lucy considered gratuitous. She said snakeroot was no good for typhoid and missionaries were no good for anything, and they had a sharp argument about it.

Indeed Lucy would often be quarrelsome from tensions at which he could not guess. "You are a neurasthenic type," he said thoughtfully one day, seeking an excuse for her snappishness. Lucy turned on him and slapped his face—a stinging blow.

He stared at her, furious, his eye watering. "You little slut!" he said, for he had learned her idiom. "What do you mean—"

"Don't you call me long names like that!"

"Slut," he observed, she hadn't resented. "You're behaving ridiculously."

"Maybe. But how should I know what curses you quacks wrap up in those jawbreakers."

"Neurasthenic," he explained, "only means subject to nervous debility."

Lucy didn't care for this either—her trumpet nostrils batted. And at bottom, he realized, she resented all his scientific knowledge; it denied her older wisdom.

But he banked a tidy sum each week from the sales

of the tonic, and that had a noticeably soothing effect on their edgy tempers. Like the account, his infatuation for Lucy grew; on a different plane it rode him as hard as ever Sinkinda had. He lavished their new wealth on her, pretty shawls, striped India lawns, blue silk gloves, and a lace parasol. He bought her a brooch which delighted him as much as it did her—a circle made of a green enamel serpent with a ruby-crusted head and tail. These feminine fineries lent his rooms a delicious frivolity that impressed on him anew how austere and ill-lighted his house of life had been.

One evening they sat talking in Timothy's room, he in his old armchair, Lucy on a little rosewood sofa with a charmingly carved frame which was part of the new furniture they had bought for the house. It was a warm evening; she had undressed and half sat, half lay in a beguiling lassitude against the black material with which the oval panels were tufted. He observed with pleasure how the dainty sofa perfectly held and suited her small round limbs, her pale flesh. For all his admiration, his acceptance of Lucy's utterly natural behavior, he still regarded nakedness as sinful and enjoyed it as such. He noticed, however, that she wore a set of jewelry he had not seen before. "That's an odd outfit," he said dubiously, for it gave her a distinctly primitive appearance. "Where did it come from?"

"Oh, it's just a little evening set a friend gave me." Lucy pushed the bracelet up on her arm, felt the earrings a trifle self-consciously.

It was the first time she had mentioned having a

170

friend who gave her things. Timothy leaned over and fingered the necklace. It was made of little dangles—ten of them—bleached and polished like ivory; they hung from a chain, two long ones in the middle, the others growing shorter at the sides.

"The design is rather pretty," he said grudgingly, and could not help adding with base appeal, "Rubies are far handsomer, don't you think?"

Lucy's eyes slid mischievously from side to side. "All is not gold that glitters," she pronounced, for she had also learned Timothy's idiom and often used it to annoy him. "The true worth of an object is not its cost in money, but its spiritual value."

"But what's its great value to you then?" cried Timothy jumping up and walking about the room. "It must be very precious for you to be flaunting it here!"

"Well, if you must know, it's an amulet—of saint's toes. A witch doctor gave it to me to ward off worldly temptations. I wear them to keep me from forgetting that I belong to another order and have a power that this dallying with you, my duck, almost makes me lose sight of." She pulled him down beside her and kissed him, half laughing, half loving.

Timothy pushed her away violently, all his jealousy of her other life frothing up in him—that mysterious, knowing life from which he was shut out.

"It seems to me, my dear Lucy, that the time has come for you to tell me a little more about yourself. Surely you can trust me, surely I have a right to know how you spend your time when you're away from me."

171

Lucy brushed aside his question. "Right? You have no right to question me about my life. We just belong to different orders of beings, and you knew that from the start."

Timothy resumed his walking. "But that's what I don't understand. What order do I belong to—the good or the bad, the Saved or the Damned? It's hellishly awkward not to know. If I'm Saved, somebody ought to tell me—if I'm Damned, I belong to your people, and I might as well have the fun of belonging. Besides, Lucy! I hate whatever divides me from you!" And throwing himself down on the sofa, he covered her with despairing kisses.

His honest passion moved her. She returned his caresses and said fondly, "Does it matter so much to you —that you should belong with me?"

"Nothing else matters."

"Well, I'll see what can be done, darling. You can't get into Satan's presence any more easily than into Heaven, you know. But I think you're almost ready to come over to us . . . if he finds you worthy there may be an opening among the werewolves, hobgoblins, or bull-beggars—I'll have to inquire."

"I'd rather be an alchemist," Timothy objected; "it's a more dignified calling."

"You'll have to be content with small beginnings, I imagine. First of all, he will have to grant you an interview."

Timothy was in transports. "Will I really come to

172

see him at last? And the throne of Satan! Oh, Lucy, Lucy! When can we go?"

"Have patience, my would-be wizard," she said, biting his ear. But she was sweeter and more loving to him than ever before.

When she left him she said, "I won't come again for a while. The moon is waxing now, there are places I have to go in the evenings."

"Lucy! Don't abandon me—"

Smiling, she tied on her shawl. "Wait," she said and, bending her head toward his, laid her finger softly on his lips.

Part Three

TIMOTHY passed the following days in a lather of impatience. He trotted to the Library and read furiously to distract his mind from the tension that mounted in him. He delved into accounts of early religions and the writings of saints and philosophers, but in his hasty mood he found them rather repetitious. Furthermore, his present way of life made their strict asceticism repellent, and he turned again to the Bible for its resplendent sinners. He did not have the temerity to own a Bible, but he assumed that the publishers of Heaven could not object to his reading it at the Library. With the aid of a concordance he looked up all references to the throne of Satan, the throne of Iniquity, Beelzebub, familiar spirits, and took notes—wishing to be well armed with congenial conversation when the great day should come.

In the course of this research he came across the lines that had given him his start in life, as he now thought of it: "I know where thou dwellest, even where Satan's throne is," and learned to his surprise that there was more of the verse—a lot about martyrdom stoically endured, which altered the meaning and was quite malapropos as far as he was concerned. For he had endured his martyrdom from habit and conformity, not stoicism. . . . He sat back in his chair, stuck out his long black-trousered legs, and gazed dismally at his toes. Had he read a little further that night—had he understood the Word differently—what *would* the outcome have been? Are our profoundest beliefs, the courses of our lives, bent by such accidents? He drew a long shuddering sigh, then sat up so suddenly his chair screeched on the floor— But of course not! The Spirit had stopped his moving finger there, at the place significant for him. The more he thought about it, the clearer the guiding hand became.

Rebounding from this shock and its implications, he vexed himself with trying to imagine what it would be like down there, and he longed to ask Lucy what was the proper deportment for such an audience, and whether or not to wear his oxblood vest. But Lucy, good as her word, came near him neither by day nor by night. He took to skulking in a little abandoned churchyard opposite her house to watch for her comings and goings, but if she went night-traveling, his eyes had no skill to see her. Still, these surroundings soothed him; the moon came there, peaked at first, then growing companionably plump; by its swelling light he could see the grassy hummocks and their eloquent headstones, and the tall pondering trees. Timothy pondered also, on mortality, on the cobweb between death and life, between fantasy and reality. He began to think he heard faint stirrings underground from those dead men, dried and packed away like herrings. Men who had been lovers, no doubt, like himself and had watched, solitary, a light in a window; who might even have lolled like him, wrapped in a dark cloak, on a lichened slab. He feared them a little, too, and luxuriated in his fear; when a snarling beetle bumped into him he started, his blood leapt in a tremor of sepulchral pleasure. He passed long hours thus, staunching his longing for Lucy, assuaging that plague of lovers—doubt when the beloved does not come. He steeped himself in a dreaming passion and went home as shriveled and black as a tea leaf.

When at last one evening he saw Lucy slipping through his garden, he halted transfixed by the window. All his blood tingled in his veins; then it stirred painfully and began to course again. By the time she had mounted the steps and come into the hall, he had covered his expectancy with calm. He kissed her quite naturally—his mind, he found, was clearer and more rational than in many weeks. They sat in the study for a while and talked about the garden and how Partridge's Hirsutus was selling, and it was all so much within the bounds of the usual that when she smiled at him and said, "What do you say to a little excursion?" he felt only a faint incredulity.

Lucy got up and went along the shelves selecting a jar, a bottle, here and there. She had brought other necessities, he observed, in her basket, and taking his arm, she went upstairs with him to his room. Timothy opened the shutters and together they looked out; the moon glinted on the eaves, and little hissings and scratchings came from among the dormers beyond their range of vision.

"They are there waiting for us," said Lucy; "you will have an escort on your aerial tour." And she looked deep into his eyes, he did not know whether with love or menace or something new, immediately to be experienced.

They drew back into the room. By the pale glare of the moonlight on the floor Timothy saw her take off her dress, and, looking tiny in her short chemise, begin to rub herself with unguents from the jars. The pupils of her eyes grew large, the irises glassy blue. Now and then she nibbled a leaf or a root. He could faintly see her flesh reddening and her hair turning tawny as it lifted along her back. His own flesh was creeping and behaving quite strangely, but he was in for it now. He felt a stab of oblique joy at finding Sinkinda before him again.

"So it comes about that we ride side by side this evening, dear Timothy." She held out a little brazen vessel that shone in the faint light. "This one comes first—but do take off your absurd sack suit; it's too cumbersome for night-traveling, and as for that horse collar—"

Timothy stripped himself to his undershirt and long cotton drawers, but these he clung to from a last-ditch

180

propriety. He boldly scooped the ointment from the jar and rubbed it on his face, arms, and legs. Immediately he felt a sharp burning and prickling through his body. Stramonium, he thought automatically, and continued to rub it on in spite of its painful effects. Mixed with frogs and newts, no doubt—*Pulv. amphibiae,* eh? But what of it. Sinkinda was holding out other jars and vials; he rubbed and nibbled hardily; the juice of one of them was particularly sharp and corrosive, his vision became blurred, and he thought he recognized solanum. Of course, if we gorm ourselves up with drugs that produce hallucinations and general vascular excitement—, he said to himself a little peevishly, for his skin was on fire. But he did not speak aloud, knowing that this apothecary's mood was out of place, and besides he was beginning to feel very queer indeed. All his flesh seemed loose and soluble; it had no more weight than a sponge, and his hair was standing erect on his head.

"Come!" exclaimed Sinkinda, seizing his hand, and with the simplest grace she started up the chimney.

Timothy tried to copy her fluid movements and went after her. Thanks to his distinguished narrowness, he rose quite easily through the vent, and in a twinkling they stood side by side on the ridgepole of the house. From such an eminence they had an unparalleled outlook. The sky was a noble blue; the silver orb filled the visible and capacious world with a fine sharp dust that crusted the harbor, the white piazzas of the sleeping town, the tiles at their feet. It was a night to make the solidest citizen fly off the ground, and Timothy's heart blew like a feather to be out with Sinkinda and the other spirits whom he now saw flying between him and the moon.

They seemed to be both male and female, and from them came a high random sound of singing. Two or three whistled down and alighted on the ridgepole— a youth whose jaws had a long wolfish angle, a girl in a skirt of snakeskin, translucent and crackling, and an indeterminate creature with one curly horn.

They shrieked to Sinkinda, whose eyes, turned on the moon, glowed cool like an animal's. Then they all, Timothy joining in, took hands along the ridgepole and began to repeat a charm: *Ab-gab-hur-huz . . . Ab-gab-hur-huz.* Timothy repeated it after them, though at first it made him think of the backs of the Encyclopedia in the bookcase at home; but when he had said it often enough it gathered magic. Suddenly the werewolf threw his head back and howled, "I'm for the air!" They all held their arms up. "Ride high!" they cried together, and flinging loose one another's hands, they slid down the steep roof and took off into the dusty moonshine.

Slowly Timothy swung his arms back for the leap— only pride gave him the final push. He shot down the slope, the gentle upturn of the bell-shaped roof lifted him slightly at the edge, a helpful start. When he felt the roof no longer under him he began to flap and kick furiously; the dark trees below rushed at him then swerved away, he found he had banked and was going up again. Little gray creatures darted over and under him and rattled him frightfully; but he saw Sinkinda, maned like a comet, shooting ahead, and he pumped after her for all he was worth.

When he had got used to the rushing noise in his ears he began to notice a sound that seemed to come out of the moon, a vibrato that thrummed all through his body. It lifted him, relaxed his tight muscles, and dissolved his fear. He looked down and saw the town laid out in flat, subaqueous hues, the rounded treetops soft with sleep pressing against the pale columns and the tiny dark windows. Only the steeples stood up alert from the lightly rocking waters; far sunken chimes hinted at wakefulness there. He could imagine St. Michael's holding its grave nightly colloquy with St. Philip's, giving out as the elder spire the law and the prophets, while St. Philip's answered with a sulky one-eyed stare of its steeple light. The earth voices, the human habitations, fell down as he mounted, and now only the bright light shrilled on the sea, joining the sound of singing in the air.

They were flying high in a great company; and meeting a cloud bank in the west, they dived through like dolphins and came out on a wide floor as if they had changed worlds. The stars, red, yellow, and blue, swung in a circle, making sharp and delicate patterns; he glanced up and found himself looking straight into the eye of the demon star, Algol, trailed by its dark follower. His companions shouted a salutation and began to weave a freakish Maypole dance about their own delegate in the starry host. Timothy lost all sense of direction, but he didn't care now whether the poles kept their places or not. He began to flap in long dignified strokes, trying to fly like a heron; he banked gracefully to the strong puffs of wind and headed up, his legs trailing. A hag swooped by him black as a bat, screeching with laughter, but he didn't allow this discourtesy to shake his self-confidence.

After a while he noticed that the others were forming in a downward spiral, and he tagged along, keeping as close to Sinkinda as his clumsy technique permitted. Gradually they approached the radiant cloudy floor again—"Like miles and miles of puffed muslin," he said, imagining that the simile was his own.

He suddenly thought of Will—little did that old buffalo guess when he recommended a voyage, a change of scene . . . Blissfully they plunged through the clouds, a delicious tingling bathed their limbs. On the nether side all was dark, they went down rapidly, the earth formed in the void, trees and water separated, each taking its own shape. Just above the treetops they flew round three times, making the magic circle, Timothy supposed—and immediately he saw a building among the thick branches, a steep-pitched roof beset with sharp finials and a short wooden belfry. The demons ahead were already settling and entering the high-pointed arch of a double doorway from which came a stream of solemn light.

"Is this a *church?*" cried Timothy, scandalized, and,

thrusting his feet out before him, he backed air hard with his arms.

"Don't be a fool!" Sinkinda swished past him. "Our architects like the ecclesiastical style, too. Stop dawdling now—and keep close to me."

Timothy, morally upset, made a rough landing but kept his feet and followed Sinkinda under the arch, which was edged with elaborately cut wooden trim. They crossed a vaulted porch and entered the great hall from which the light streamed.

What a lofty building, thought Timothy. Like the Crystal Palace, only better. In the hall itself lancet windows of stained glass streamed with light, presumably artificial. The far wall was oval; against it a wide staircase swirled up to a gallery that ran around the hall some thirty feet above their heads. And above this still the shadowy cavity went up and up to the sharp angle of the roof. There a skylight, also of stained glass, was set in, through which the moon shone brightly and shot the hall and stair with jeweled colors.

"Great heavens, but this is a handsome apartment," Timothy whispered to Sinkinda. "The Dev— that is, the Adversary—is a man of superlative taste, I should say."

Sinkinda's eyebrows rounded. "The Adversary? Be careful of your terms, my dear man. From where you stand now, the Adversary is the Other One. Remember everything is relative, and don't make faux pas."

"But what shall I call him?"

185

"That depends," said Sinkinda unsatisfactorily, and began to talk to old friends who crowded round to admire her, for all the world like Penny's coterie at the church door.

Words, then, were even more tricky in Hell than at home. Timothy resolved to have as little to do with them as possible and gave his attention to the guests.

The assemblage before him had a brilliant international flavor. Witches from all parts of the world, wizards of the North in pointed hats, dwarfs, giants, hobgoblins from all the islands in Time . . . they milled about the hall, roosted on the balcony rail above, or drifted up and down the staircase while the blue and red gleams shimmered on them as if the skylight itself were moving. Their long predatory fingernails gave out a faint clashing sound, and as they made the turn of the staircase their eyes shone for a moment with the cold fauna gleam that denied both pity and rational argument.

This noise is deafening, he said to himself, it's like receptions at home—and in answer to his thought a bell-boy stood at his elbow with some tufts of cotton wool. Timothy put them in his ears, wondering how much he should tip the fellow. But he had no pocketbook, nor even a pocket, which solved the problem.

At that moment he began to have a queer feeling. A young vampire had slipped up beside him, and some compass needle within him began to jump and run wild. He stood stock-still and looked at her out of one eye like a rooster; then he shuddered with joy, because

186

she had the romantic and sensual beauty that men invent in their dreams. She swung round and faced him and he thought she said, Come with me . . . but perhaps not, since the lissome swaying of her body as she began to move backward made words superfluous. Timothy followed her avidly, yet with nightmare dragging at his feet, for through his bewitchment he saw that her lips were vermilion and her curved nails like clots of blood. He didn't know whether he was angry or relieved when Sinkinda bore down on them, steam coming out of her nostrils, and snatched him bodily away.

The vampire showed fight, and Timothy backed under the staircase until the ladies should settle their differences. They clawed each other swiftly, they threw back their heads and seemed to utter uninhibited screeches, but the cotton in his ears spared him this terrible sound. It was skillfully medicated, he observed, to shut out only offensive noises. I must find out this ingenious formula for the future—if I have a future, he thought.

The fight was proceeding in a manner that offended his sense of sportsmanship, and he took advantage of Sinkinda's preoccupation to stroll off a little and do some sightseeing on his own.

The first and most startling sight to confront him was himself; he stopped short, hypnotized. He was looking into a tall narrow mirror set between two windows and bonneted with rococo gilt. His undershirt and long drawers had collected a coating of soot in his trip up the chimney and had shrunk to fit him tightly like a ballet costume. His skin showed the dark stain he saw on all the others. It relieved him greatly to find that he had not dropped in on this assemblage in plain underwear; indeed, with his black suit, his pale flowing hair, his distinguished angularity, he looked quite fiendish, he thought, and very fine.

He could have spent some time admiring his own appearance but Sinkinda, victrix, came up and appropriated the mirror. She produced a comb from her bosom and fluffed out her touseled bang, she backed off, studying herself with impassioned appraisal, she smoothed and plucked at her filmy skirt of long mauve petals. Advancing again she all but got into the mirror while she repaired from her pomatum jar three or four long gashes made by the vampire's nails. "Have you had a look around? I hope it lives up to your expectations. You earthlings are pretty exacting in your ideas of Hell."

"It's beautiful," said Timothy with honest awe. "So spacious, so rich, so nobly proportioned."

"Of course. It has room for everybody . . . eventually. And now Satan is ready to see you. Come this way."

She led Timothy across the hall to a pair of sliding doors that parted hospitably for them. He found himself in a sort of study with an alcove opening at one side. At a desk against the opposite wall the Archfiend sat, leaning his familiar saturnine face reflectively on his hand; his person, buttoned into a frock coat, was groomed and glossy, his black hair grew in a widow's peak on his low forehead. On the whole, Timothy

188

thought, astounded, he looked very much like a Charlestonian. He rose and civilly held out his hand as they approached.

"Good evening, Dr. Partridge; we are happy to have you with us, I'm sure."

Timothy said, "I am indeed happy to be here, sir," in a rather squeaky tenor.

"You couldn't have come under better auspices, I may say." Satan bowed courteously towards his companion.

Sinkinda, Timothy observed with surprise, lost her superb confidence on coming into the Presence. She smiled at Satan almost coyly, she assumed serpentine poses, she smoldered at him from her covert of hair. But the Master seemed unimpressed by her wiles. "Be seated, I beg of you." He resumed his place in his armchair. "I've heard of your interest in our philosophy and practices; I hope you will feel quite at home here. I am going to be rather busy, but some of my relations will show you about." Timothy murmured his thanks for this exceptional courtesy and Satan went on. "You must see the Library. Our collection is complete, I believe; we have first editions of all the works on magic by the practitioners of the art, including many saints and scientists. I keep the incunabula here." He waved a long rubbery hand sporting a handsome onyx ring toward the alcove lined with shelves of books.

"Timothy is more interested in potions," said Sinkinda. "He has quite a few customers now. I am hoping he will bring you converts, sir." She leaned on

189

the desk and looked at Satan with something akin to doting in her self-possessed features. Timothy felt a pang . . . and yet it won't do, he thought, to be jealous of the Devil. . . .

"Ah?" said Satan. "Well, have a look about, Partridge, you'll find much to interest you. My line of poisons is unsurpassed. For instance, in the alcove here . . ."

Satan rose and went through the arch. After an inquiring glance at Sinkinda, Timothy followed. The alcove contained a terrestrial and a celestial globe and a crystal gazing ball; the book-filled shelves, he saw, were cleverly painted to simulate the grain of oak.

With boyish proprietorship Satan went about touching secret springs in the panels; the sections revolved and showed their reverse sides, which proved to be more shelves filled with jars, bottles, phials, and limbecks. Little pointed arches of dark wood framed the top row—in short, Timothy almost thought his beloved shop had been snatched from the burning and set up here. Satan touched the jars with graceful indifference: "Mandrake, hemlock, wolfsbane—a really pure alkaloid and therefore one of the finest poisons in nature." He moved along to the patent medicine section and, taking down a bottle, offered it to Timothy. "L'Elixir d'Amour—" He sent a sly glance toward Sinkinda. "I believe you sold an imitation in your pharmacy. Here our drugs are unadulterated. But I can show you an even better trick." He picked up a jar and a spatula and began skillfully to compound some unguent. In a few minutes his cuffs and the front of his coat were spattered and dusty.

In these surroundings Satan looked so natural a pharmacist that Timothy gave a startled glance at the man's feet and was relieved to see that while one foot was neatly encased in patent leather the other wore an iron shoe, obviously to correct a deformity.

Unluckily Satan appeared to tire of puddling ointments before he had revealed the exceptional formula. He brushed off his clothes and said, "Look here, Partridge, there are some questions I want to ask you."

They returned to the study and resumed their seats. The heavy desk stood between them like a judgment bar. Timothy began to ooze perspiration; the study, he noticed, was intolerably hot and stuffy. The heat seemed to be coming from an elaborately wrought grille which pierced one wall; through it he saw red flickerings and heard long-drawn dismal cries which his ear plugs only partially muffled. Goose bumps broke out on his arms and neck.

Satan observed his predicament and frowned slightly. He rose, went over to the grille and listened for a moment, then he shouted, "That will do for today— bank the fires!" Turning back, he remarked, "Our heating system is the most effective ever invented, and very cheap to operate," and he courteously placed an embroidered fire screen between Timothy and the grille.

Going behind the desk, he stood for a moment leaning lightly on his knuckles and fixed on Timothy a remarkably fine pair of black eyes. Then, in a voice charged with menace and summoning, he said, "Dr. Partridge, do you believe in God?"

Timothy sat paralyzed. He glanced in anguish at Sinkinda, but her smoky eyes were depthless. What'll I do? he said to himself, hearing a dry rattle as if his entrails had shriveled in the fires beneath and were knocking about inside his crawling skin. Yet a kind of mettle pulsed there under the fatty tissues of caution. Though Satan's imps tear him in pieces . . . He closed his eyes and said in a big voice, "Yes, sir."

"Capital!" cried Satan. "A well-spoken man, Sinkinda. He passes the first test with flying colors."

Timothy opened his eyes, but in his fright they wouldn't focus. Satan and Sinkinda whirled about him in confusion. Presently he found his tongue. "Oh . . . I thought . . . I supposed . . ."

"No doubt you did. You've been brought up on heretical ideas by divines who will stop at nothing to accomplish my disreputation. Those sermons of theirs? Winter's tales and old wives' fables! Why, I hate an atheist above everything. The stubborn, stiff-necked, gristly vermin—the world should be rid of them!"

His vehemence loosened two locks of hair, which stood up, charmingly pointed, from his forehead. He smoothed them down with both palms and went on. "Obviously I can exist only if the Adversary exists: what impudence to deny us! The unbeliever, my friend, sterilizes—denatures—life. Besides, as a practical matter"

—he spread his hands and appealed to Timothy with manly reasonableness—"unless people believe in some Good they have no sense of guilt in doing wrong and therefore offer me no hold."

"Naturally . . . of course not," said Timothy, mustering his wits as best he could. His intentions seemed to be acceptable, for Satan drew a box of Havanas from his desk and offered Timothy one. From another box he took a small twisted black cigar for Sinkinda: "A brand especially affected by Russian countesses," he said, smiling, and, cracking his knuckles, lighted it for her from a spark.

"Ah, Magister—" Sinkinda murmured, giving him a sultry look from under her great golden fluff.

In a moment they were all puffing away, and Timothy thought he had never been in more congenial surroundings than this handsome study with its rich dark draperies and polished wood, its brilliant and agreeable company. Presently Satan said, "Now perhaps there are some questions you would like to ask me."

As usual, Timothy's list of conversational topics treacherously eluded him. He pulled himself together, however, and made a stab at it. "Tell us a little more about Good and Evil, sir. If you would vouchsafe some enlightenment on that plaguing question—" He hesitated; what he really wanted to ask, namely, had man any hope of rooting out Evil, seemed less than tactful. He went on: "People's good qualities are so often bad;

the well-meaning do as much mischief as the wicked—
and yet you have to have the good will, the good intention—" He paused, treading water.

"But, my dear man, you exercise yourself quite un-
necessarily about that sort of thing. Good and Evil
are interactive—they depend on each other for existence. Which camp you prefer is largely a matter of
taste."

"But that philosophy just won't do," said Timothy
inflammably. "In the end you have to have a moral
order, a reason for a course of action. Even you admit
that to sin you have to have a code to sin against."

"True enough," said Satan, "and if it's morals you're
after, I've a great lumber room full of them, collected
down the ages. You might look them over and see if
any of them suits your fancy. Some are very quaint and
curious."

"But what I want to know is, will any of them stick?"
cried Timothy in anguish. "Are there any you can
get your teeth into? Besides, there's another, a personal,
question that hangs on this: Am I Saved or am I
Damned? I can't even find that out!"

Satan smiled and blew three perfect rings before he
answered. "You must ask my Opponent about that. He
has a perfect mania for saving and damning. I should
guess your prospects were poor. The Damned have a
rough time of it, I fear." He glanced mockingly toward
the grille. "I invite you to avoid all that unpleasantness
by joining us voluntarily. We have our Immortals in
Hell, too, you know; I could use you as an emissary

to the world to bring in recruits—your knowledge of alchemy would come in quite handy. Indeed, I may as well confess to having put an inconspicuous mark on you back in the winter. There's a nice position open among the enchanters—a most amusing profession, I promise you! Think it over. But now my presence is demanded elsewhere; the important part of our little celebration is about to take place. Sinkinda, see to it that Dr. Partridge has a good seat and whatever comforts he may require. It is a great pleasure to have you here, sir, let me assure you." He bowed with old-world courtesy and came from behind the desk.

Before Timothy could take his outstretched hand Sinkinda seized it and devoutly kissed the great onyx ring. Satan smiled with paternal condescension and pinched her ear. Then he pushed a panel in the wall and disclosed a shining cage which he entered, turning about to face the door. The ropes inside slatted, the Archfiend began to descend in brass-framed majesty, the panel slowly closed upon his reverse assumption.

"Whew!" said Timothy, "What next, old girl? I declare, they do put on a show in this place!"

Sinkinda darted a surprised look at him, and indeed these familiarities astounded Timothy himself. But this visit to Hell was improving his sense of proportion in several ways.

"He has gone to dress for the Audience. We must hurry if you're going to get a good seat."

Timothy took a last look around to impress the room on his memory, intending to carry home a few ideas for his own house. Suddenly he exclaimed in dismay, "But the throne, Sinkinda! That cane-bottomed armchair can't be the throne of Satan!"

"In Satan's house are many mansions," said Sinkinda loftily. "Have patience, my duck, you're still a rank amateur."

The hall was full of bustle when they returned to it. The guests, sufficiently odd to start with, flopped in and out of weird costumes; it all looked rather like a backstage scene at a performance of high school theatricals. Some imps slid screaming down the banisters of the tall, perilous stairway and roused a juvenile envy in Timothy, but Sinkinda threaded her way steadfastly between them, towing him after her. They went through a low door and along a tunnel, at the end of which they climbed a circular stair and came out on a sort of musicians' gallery overlooking the audience chamber.

Timothy stopped short, his normal sense of scale knocked spinning. The huge room was half dark; the groined roof hung pale above them like thunderheads changed to stone. Occult symbols in brass studded the floor in gleaming asymmetrical scrolls as if an enormous snake had thrown its skin the length of the room to the wide gray curtain at its far bounds.

As he stood there in amaze, several people rushed past him for the front row. "Timothy!" cried Sinkinda sharply, and beckoned him to the railing. He stumbled down the steps and took the chair she was holding for him. "Don't be a ninny," she muttered, "and hang on to it with both hands; these people will stop at nothing to get a front seat. You have to look sharp and move fast," she said, "if you are going to survive around here. Now keep your eyes open, and if there's any flim-flam doing, you do it. I must go now—I'll meet you after the Audience."

The great chandeliers began to bud and slowly to bloom, drawing out with theatrical genius the moment of anticipation. People sifted in through the low-arched doors on either side the hall and soon filled it, but softly, dustily, as if robbed of substance by their awe. A thunderclap crashed on Timothy's ears; the lights blazed up. The curtain at the far end shivered through its velvet length and majestically drew apart in operatic loops. Between them he saw the canopied seat on the dais. Both throne and dais were of basalt, and on the seven steps on each side stood seven attendant demons dressed in red and silver. It was all just as he had imagined it and incredibly satisfying, except that the severely plain black stone gave off a grim sheen. The throne itself was still empty. It looked quite uncomfortable, he thought—no upholstery or anything. However, he didn't mean to be critical, so he hung over the balustrade and stared at the Ring of Trumpeters in heraldic dress that had formed before the dais. Setting their long trumpets to their lips, they blew a cacophonous blast, and in a twinkling the Monarch himself stood in the ring in his robes of state. A long "Ah . . ." went up from the crowd; Satan turned a little from side to side, not recognizing his myrmidons but merely showing himself in his long jeweled mantle. The Ring of Trumpeters opened behind him and he turned and walked up to the throne.

The rout below was forming in a sort of unruly procession, each demon with his own kind. A wild, syncopated music began to throb, pumped into the hall from openings in the walls; and to these strains the first tribe moved up to the throne, singing and hailing Satan as Beelzebub, Prince of the East. The worshipers had the proper air of oriental splendor . . . the Magicians of Egypt in their black and silver capes, sinewy Nubians leading leopards on braided leashes, Philistines with sharp-pointed red beards. The brazen vessels they carried filled the air with sweet smoke from aromatic woods. Beelzebub's robes were magenta, Timothy saw, embroidered with pink and red—a somewhat garish selection for his Western tastes; the gold looked brassy, and everyone seemed overdressed. Still . . .

Other groups surged in behind. Sifting the crowd carefully, he spied Sinkinda wearing a long Babylonish dress in which she appeared taller, more imposing than in the dark green habit she wore for business. Her hair crimped into narrow little braids hung like gold fringe round her head. The sight of her walking haggard and seductive in the galaxy pinched his heart—what a lucky man I am, he thought, almost with tears.

Satan himself seemed to be changing his appearance in the manner of a dream. The jeweled mantle had disappeared, a black velvet suit of antique style set off the incredible grace of his limbs. His finely shaped calves shone in silk; Lucifer's emblem, the daystar, winked in his peaked cap; and he looked down with smiling condescension as the array of witches, wizards, werewolves, and alchemists accompanying Sinkinda prostrated themselves before him. Her party had brought its animals too, among which Timothy especially noticed a brindled cat, splendid in amber and black, and playing a fiddle.

As the rout pressed forward Timothy became confused; at one point he thought he identified his friends the Manichaeans by the elaborate fire effects they set off. The music pounded and throbbed, the worshipers jostled and fought for place. They made way, however, for a group of necromancers carrying skeletons and trailed by ghouls and ghosts that looked unpleasantly dead—a malodorous crew, Timothy deduced, from the way the others sheered off from them.

The spectators in the gallery shrieked to their friends below; the din became frenzied—in spite of the cotton in his ears he began to feel beaten to pulp; so it was with relief that he saw what appeared to be the lowest order of spirits take their place before the throne . . . a rabble of fortunetellers, creatures on broomsticks, boo-hags, boo-daddies, and the commoner kinds of satyrs, accompanied by goats, black dogs, and bats. The Master had graciously altered his appearance to suit their rusticity; uninhibited, he waved a fine long tail; his cloven foot, unshod, pawed the dais slightly, his horns stuck jauntily through two holes in his hat; in short, it was Old Scratch himself. Suddenly Timothy wished for

Maum Rachel. How she would have loved it all—the
color, the theatrical effects, the parade of celebrities!

The unmistakable smell of flowers of brimstone
accompanied this category of spirits; a fine yellow powder filled the air and made Timothy's throat burn.
Coughing, he pushed back his chair, jostled his way out
of the gallery, and went down the winding staircase.
In the corridor below he became even more confused;
dark tunnels he hadn't noticed before led away on
either side. He ran into one blind alley after another.
He thought he could hear the revelers trampling out of
the great hall; Sinkinda's voice wove tantalizingly
through the noise, and, calling her name in a despairing
shout, he beat on the wall before him. It crumpled like
cardboard, and he stumbled forward from his own
momentum into a large sort of dressing room, or so
he gathered, since it was full of diabolical ladies repair-
ing their make-up before the mirrors. At his sudden
appearance they all screamed with laughter.

"Oh, I beg your pardon . . . I didn't dream . . . there
must be some mistake . . ." Paralyzed with embarrass-
ment, he backed towards the rent he had made in the
rose-garlanded wallpaper with which the room was
hung.

But Sinkinda pushed through the group and took
his arm. "Come in, Timothy, and join the ladies. No
prudes here, my pet. I'd like to have you meet my
friends." She presented Timothy to some of the best-
known witches, Hecate and the Weird Sisters, the Witch
of Scrapfaggot Green, and Sidonia the Sorceress—who

once had done away with the entire ducal house of Hanover. Timothy began to recover his aplomb; he made a leg and murmured civilly, "I've always wanted to meet you, ma'am . . . delighted, I'm sure . . ." He was not even put off when a tall, astonishingly thin witch to whom he held out his hand drew herself up even taller, bent over into a hoop, and rolled across the room without speaking to him, for he recognized Sycorax, whose reputation for bad manners had been long exploited by playwrights.

As a group they did not appeal to Timothy. Wrinkles creased their sharp-featured faces, without make-up their moles and birthmarks showed, their hair needed washing. But their wit was nimble, racy, full of the charm of the unexpected; and some, like Sinkinda and Sidonia, were handsome and accomplished.

They stared unblushingly at Timothy and even fingered his person in a manner that disconcerted him extremely; they asked embarrassing questions, which Sinkinda was kind enough to answer for him. She had found him refreshingly free, she added, from the bigotry and prejudice that dogged witches—indeed, he had plagued the life out of her to bring him here. The ladies seemed delighted with this account of him and only Sinkinda's proprietary snarls when they pressed too close saved him, Timothy divined, from learning more about Evil than he had quite bargained for.

He put his lips to Sinkinda's ear. "Confound it, get me away from here before—"

Sinkinda herself seemed to think it was about time.

"Move aside, girls, and let us out; you'll have to go find your own gentlemen just as I did." And she threw back her head and made a sound like a cock crowing.

The witches winced, they fell back, suddenly gray. "What? Morning . . . ? Already . . . ?" In the break thus made, Sinkinda rushed Timothy across the room and through the door. Back in the great entrance hall, she shouted with glee at the success of her ruse. "They are really ridiculous," she said, "ridden with superstition. Look—the dance is beginning. Let's go and join in."

Deeply chagrined, Timothy had to confess that he had never learned to dance. Sinkinda received the news peevishly. "Oh, those puritanical sects! They are always mixing religion and manners and morals in a holy mess. Why can't they learn that they are all separate, really? Too bad, you'll have to miss the best part of the evening." Brusquely she dropped his arm and slipped away into the crowd.

Considerably put out, Timothy decided to find his own amusements. He picked his way across the hall with difficulty, for the revelers were spinning and whirling now, entangled with the younger imps playing anagrams on the floor. Some of these got up and made a rush for an archway Timothy had noticed earlier. The sliding doors had remained closed all evening, and, prompted by sheer curiosity, he fell in behind the imps as they parted them and pushed through the opening. He had time, however, for only a glimpse of a weirdly furnished interior when the last imp turned on him and, shouting, "Devil take the hindermost!" seized the inside knobs and slammed the doors in his face.

Timothy glanced involuntarily over his shoulder, but no Satanic personage stood by. The dancers continued their hypnotized swaying unaware of his existence. Damn those brats—he hadn't expected such childish display in this sophisticated resort; but adolescents were the same everywhere, no doubt. He scrutinized the doors; the desire to see what he wasn't meant to put heart in him; he seized the silver knobs and pulled the doors a little apart.

He stuck his head in the crack and took a quick look around. "Great Scott!" he exclaimed, and slammed the doors again. Obscenity he could not get used to.

A throaty chuckle beside him caught his ear. A short, obese man was sitting against the wall, his excess fat pouching over the edges of his chair. He had a sleek head shaped like a melon and he held a wand or divining rod above the floor as if searching for water or precious metals.

"There is entertainment in this place to suit all tastes," he remarked. "I expect what you'd like to see is the lumber room where the morals are in storage. I got word to direct you there if you want to go."

"Oh . . . why, thank you—how very kind—" Timothy took another look at the man, whose fine slanting dark eyes suggested that if a hundred pounds or so were pared off him he would bear the stamp of the royal family. He wore a robe of some gold fabric made in an

203

antique style, and all his pudgy fingers were covered to the knuckles with rings. To be on the safe side Timothy bowed, and murmured, "I am honored indeed. Perhaps you'd be kind enough to show me where the lumber room is."

"Up the grand staircase, turn right, third door on the left." The man got up and pushed his way imperturbably across the hall with Timothy following in his broad wake. At the foot he paused and motioned upward. "You'll forgive me if I don't go with you . . . a steep climb . . . shortness of breath . . ." He sat down on the steps and, dipping his rod over the banisters, he angled lazily above what little floor space the dancers left him.

From the first Timothy had wanted an excuse to go up these stairs, so he mounted them nimbly, enjoying the unparalleled view their heights gave him of the revelry. Making many stops to admire the prospect and the stained glass above his head, he at length reached the gallery.

The third door on the left proved to be heavy and its lock rusty. Few of Hell's inhabitants, he supposed, bothered with what lay behind it. He shoved it open, screaming on its hinges, and let himself in. The long apartment was wan and dusty indeed after the magnificent appointments of the rest of Hell, and the air reeked with mold. Stacks and stacks of books and papers stretched away into infinity, it seemed. The light was miserable for reading, he could just make out the titles—tracts, sermons, and precepts, books of taboos, blue laws

204

and sumptuary laws—these moralists must have produced sinners right and left, he thought in astonishment. Used as he had become to the furnace heat of Hell, this attic made his teeth chatter, or else the task of hunting for a workable moral here chilled his blood, so he went out and descended the staircase again.

As he neared the bottom he looked over the banister and saw Sinkinda spinning in a kind of a saraband with a handsome young demon she had picked up. An unworthy jealousy nipped him; the demon had all of Satan's grace, but softened to the verge of sweetness, which gave his saturnine face a delicate impudicity. He might easily have been the result of one of Satan's indiscretions—the kind of chap, Timothy thought, built to Sinkinda's order. At that moment the dance brought them near; reprehensibly he leaned over the banisters and screamed in the fellow's face: "Devil's get!" The demon turned and made a half bow which he wove with clever improvisation into his pattern of steps; his narrow lips curled in a lazy acknowledgment of his distinguished origins. Then they wheeled again and Sinkinda faced him. Although she was close by, he might have been another spindle in the banisters. Her eyes devoured her partner, but as Timothy caught their pale flicker, his jealousy died within him; that impersonal possessiveness was nothing he cared to see bent on himself. He turned and went down the steps, his shoulders hunched up to his ears.

The same tranced expression had come over the other faces about him; the dance was developing into an orgy.

He edged along the wall, both relieved and disconsolate at Sinkinda's flat abandonment of him; it left him in the forlorn situation of being at a large party where he did not know anyone. His fat friend was shouldering toward the majestic portieres of an archway at the right of the stairs; he looked back and beckoned, and for want of other company Timothy shouldered after him.

He found himself in a handsomely appointed room walled around with bookshelves. It was a dream library, for the velours hangings at the doors and windows shut out all sounds; deeply upholstered chairs stood about, and the thick fringed table covers muffled even the laying down of a book. A fire burned low in the great chimney-place before which his guide stood with his gold robe tucked up, cosily warming his plump rear. Near him a great book entitled *The Damned Art* lay on a table. There was a Biblical unction about it, about the stiff age-blackened binding, the small table all its own.

As Timothy joined him at the fire the little man spoke. "Have you enjoyed your excursion here?"

"Well, yes—in a way. Certainly there is nothing more to be desired in such an apartment as this one." Timothy looked greedily about at the gleaming books, the bronze statuary, the ubiquitous fringed hangings. "But there is so much in Hell to confuse a simple apothecary . . . you have been most courteous, sir; I wonder if I may impose on you for a little information?"

"Knowledge is riches," said his guide, smiling; "never

forget that. But ask away—I'll see what I can do for you."

"In particular, Mr.— May I first make so bold as to inquire your name, sir?"

The man's fat cheeks dimpled. He said almost coyly, "My Christian name is Mammon; it's the one I like best, though I get called many names—all rich men do. Happy to see you here, sir."

They bowed courteously to each other and Timothy went on. "In particular I've been hoping to find some-one of whom I might ask a rather delicate question. Do you ever in your wanderings through Hell . . . I suppose you get about a good deal . . . see a lady . . . perhaps she isn't here at all . . . but I just thought I'd ask . . ."

"For the love of damnation, man, come to the point! We've dispensed with those pale hesitancies of speech down here. Who is this female?"

"My sister, Miss Penelope Partridge."

Mammon gave Timothy a cheerful leer. "Miss Penny Partridge, eh? Yes, I know her; though she seldom comes here, not having much taste for our revels. She's in a Hell of her own—with a few like-minded—next door there."

He nodded toward the bay window at the far end of the room. The half-drawn curtains showed a narrow strip of beautiful moonlit park where willow trees drooped over pale statues glimmering down a vista.

"Go and take a look."

Timothy slogged across the thick-piled carpet. When he parted the curtains he saw that the park was only painted on a backdrop of canvas. The hollow eyes of the nearest statue shone unnaturally brilliant, like Sinkinda's, from an external source; then he perceived that they were peepholes, lighted from beyond. He stepped hesitantly up to the naiad and applied his eyes to hers.

The apartment into which he looked was large and of an unparalleled richness; indeed, sofas, draperies, whatnots, so cluttered it that little space remained for human occupancy. It was empty at the moment, but on a near-by chair Penelope's coat lay folded with her bonnet on top as he had often seen them at home, put aside for some immediate household task. And there beside them were the badges of her servitude—a dustpan, pail, mop, and a little pile of dust and cobwebs. Hell, Timothy could only suppose, had failed to provide an adequate staff for this fine mansion of Penelope's imagining, or, more politic punishment, she lived there in slavery to her rich possessions. Other little piles of dust dotted the carpet, and now he perceived that beside each one lay a figure, a sort of clay statue minus an arm, a leg, a head, and some were ground to dust again by a heel shod with impotent fury.

At this moment Timothy felt himself elbowed aside. "Give me a peep," said Mammon, pushing his bold face into the naiad's. He stared for a few minutes while deep soundless laughter shook the muscles of his belly. "It must be Thursday. She spends all her evenings off trying to recreate the victims of her kindness; and actually the woman has become very adept, her likenesses grow better and better—she might have made a sculptress on earth. But"—he spun around cackling to share with Timothy the cream of the jest—"no matter how like they are, when she fills that deep bosom of hers and tries to breathe the breath of life into them, they crumble and fall back to dust. A refined chastisement that does credit to the Archfiend's imagination."

Timothy turned away, grieving for the lost sculptress, feeling that her fate was unduly hard—but why look for mercy here? As he walked back to the fireplace with Mammon he said pensively, "I've never quite understood about Sister and Mr. Dombie. If she had learned to bring people back from the dead, how is it that she lives here as a sinner and doesn't belong to Satan's flock—or perhaps pack is a better word for it?"

Mammon shrugged and refilled his curly-stemmed pipe. "She never took advantage of her opportunities. She was too refined and too stubborn—vices which often go in pairs, you will notice—to traffic with the Devil, so she worked out her myths and fantasies on the psychological plane. If she had come out for good, honest witchcraft, now—"

Timothy looked for a long time into the rosy embers. He sighed sentimentally. "At least she's not below in the furnace. I suppose that's something."

"That, Doctor, is for the cruder sorts of sinners. Under our social system: for the lower orders, the furnaces; for the higher organisms—and she did have a fine

209

frenzy about her—the smokeless burning of the mind. Which reminds me—the fire wants mending." He turned and shouted toward the portieres, "Hoppo! Huckle! Bring more fuel directly! The way the fires are allowed to burn low in this place is a cosmic scandal."

Two imps came in, bringing some queerly shaped lumps and bundles, and threw them on the coals. The glow sank for a few minutes, then, seizing its fresh fodder, the fire sprang up. An unpleasant smell began to creep through the apartment. Timothy did not look into the flames, because he had a nasty suspicion about the lumps. Instead he plunged headlong into conversation to choke back a slight nausea. "I must say, this is the most magnificent library. Such books! My little weakness, you know."

Mammon nodded. "All the books of mischief ever written. Like the Bodleian Library, only better. Immensely valuable, of course; many of them with the names of famous personages on their flyleaves. I could get . . . let's see . . ." His thin lips, the only straight line in his profusion of curves, narrowed as he frowned over the exact computation: ". . . about twenty-five million for them at the present rate of exchange." His little slant eyes seemed to turn red as they went over the crammed shelves, almost as if he were stripping the books to their naked silver value.

This licentiousness shocked Timothy more than anything he had seen in Hell. "I can't think of them in terms of money," he said after a pause.

Mammon's face relaxed. He laughed, all curves again.

"Never fear; no use for me to sell them. Once I had the money, I'd covet the books. I just like to go over our assets—there's a lot more satisfaction in thinking about money than in spending it, if people only knew. I see you love books genuinely. You'd find this collection unique."

"No doubt of it. I used to be a collector myself in a modest way. I had several curiosities of the literature of magic and even a few firsts."

Suavely Mammon picked up *The Damned Art* from the table where it lay. "My dear Doctor, why don't you decide now to join us and come back here in a state of grace? Then you would share our privileges, which you've hardly begun to hear about. But the choice has to be made in life, you understand; no shabby death-bed repentances, such as the Adversary accepts, will be counted here. No dissipating your life in Christian virtues and then escaping the frugalities of Heaven at the end."

Timothy said, "I could spend an eternity blissfully here, just browsing through these books." His eyes on the beckoning shelves bulged a little in a startled acceptance like the eyes of a hooked fish.

Mammon dropped his voice; he became intimate, confidential. The fat little salesman, Timothy thought, dressed up in a gold robe. "Open this book, Doctor, and read the secret of Evil. Acquire the wisdom of Hell, and whatever you may desire will be added—gratis."

Timothy looked at the book Mammon held out. Between its pages hung bookmarks of rich purple satin;

the cabalistic ornaments in silver that dangled from
their ends winked in the uneasy light. The fire-tending
imps drew near and watched him with piercing curiosity.

Did ever a man sell his soul for a plush-hung library?
he wondered—for the heady pleasures of reading? But
there was Lucy; he wanted to be with her, he remembered. It would be rather creditable, a fine romantic
gesture, to embrace Evil in order to be with his love.
And the solace it would bring his gnawing curiosity to
have this matter of Good and Evil settled! For if he
opened this book he would know Good also by simple
elimination. He ran his tongue over his dry lips.

"Give it to me."

The heavy goatskin binding had a slickness, an unc-
tuous texture, in his hands. He closed his eyes and
inserted his thumbnail between the pages while he
tried to conjure up against his dark lids the passage his
eyes would fall on. And all at once he caught a glimpse,
beyond the thick paper and the Gothic script crowding
it, of the Evil recorded there, lying in blackness under all
life, a water-table from which fountains rose and collected in foul pools in human brains. He could smell
the senseless brutality, the blood; treacheries and cor-
rupt lusts, cowardices like wharf-rats, all that was finally
unacceptable, swam in those dissolute waters. He stood
so engrossed, his eyes screwed tight in his long seeker's
face, that Mammon cried, "What! Lost your nerve,
man?" Hoppo and Huckle slapped their thighs, they

212

ran between Timothy's legs and nipped his calves with their sharp nails.

Timothy opened his eyes and looked at the book with a repugnance that gushed unimpeded now. Like Gideon tearing down the altar of Baal, he stalked between the imps and threw it into the fireplace.

An explosion shook the room, fire and black smoke belched from the chimney, they all fell back choking. Mammon began to bellow, the imps screamed like a thousand devils. The flames seized the hearth rug, the table cover, in their teeth; in a moment the near-by hangings were ablaze. With a wild backward look at the holocaust, Timothy sprang through the portieres and ran into the hall. It was empty except for some sleepy attendants, the revelers having gone on to more private enjoyments. In unashamed panic, he dashed through the great doorway and out of the building.

The darkness outside was stunning after the incandescence indoors. Half blinded, he floundered about; he flapped his arms, but the secret of flying had escaped him; he couldn't think how to rise from the ground. Vaguely he distinguished a pale streak of driveway and ran crouching along it for a little, feeling for abysses at his feet.

He had gone some distance when he heard a sound so familiar that it brought him immediate comfort, the sound of a horse cropping the grass beside the road. He quickly came upon it, a noble black animal, hitched to a light, black vehicle—or perhaps they merely looked dark against the pallor of the roadway. Groping and fumbling, he found the iron weight to which the tether was fastened, threw it into the gig, and sprang up after it. "Giddap!" he shouted, and slapped the reins on the horse's gleaming back.

With a spring that almost snapped Timothy out backward, the horse started and sped along the drive. High gateposts flashed by, the gig rushed down a dark road going somewhere very rapidly. Timothy tried to steady his thoughts against the rocking of their passage. Darkness hung overhead and on either hand and let through no clue as to their whereabouts. What sort of beast was this? A conjecture lit up his mind with the stab of a match flame: this was Satan's own gig-horse, harnessed and ready for a sudden visit to the upper world. He hung on to the reins and hoped for the best.

The first familiar sight to his eyes were some stars overhead. He seemed to have come on the outskirts of a town, but they sped too fast for him to recognize the dim houses. Timothy wondered if this beast were as sapient as he should be for such a profession, and decided to chance it. "We're going after Dr. Timothy Partridge!" he shouted. "To Dr. Partridge's house!"

Again the horse sprang forward. The streets rushed by, familiar now in flashes. Dirt, cobblestones, then more dirt; the lampposts ran up to them like link boys, and in a twinkling they came to a dead stop before Timothy's gate.

He clambered out and sat for a moment on the horse block, his legs too slack-twisted to hold him. The death-like stillness before the dawn lay on the street. The moon had long sunk, the roof from which he had started ages ago was shrouded in leaves of darkness. Tottering to his feet, Timothy wondered what he should do with his undomesticated charger. The livery stable? But it was closed. He waved his hand weakly toward the horse's head. "Good-by, old fellow—I expect you're sharp enough to get home by yourself." He wobbled along the path and up to his bed.

Part Four

$\mathcal{T}$IMOTHY woke the next day and thought—Dear God! Did I really go to Hell and burn it up? He drew a deep breath, a Messianic complacency stirred in him. The adventure had, to be sure, the wild improbability of a dream, but that didn't concern him much; the wall between dream and reality had worn as thin for him as the surrounding mosquito net. From his bolster he could see the fireplace, the slop-jar, the rosewood sofa, clearly yet pearled in the gauze; when he rose and moved among them, the figures of his fantastic world would be as pearly-clear to him as the slop-jar was now. And he was content that each world should have its own validity. So thinking, he sat up, released the patent frame; the canopy sprang back to the head of the bed and the net folded above him like a king's baldequin.

When he had breakfasted he walked out to the front gate. The black horse and gig were nowhere in sight. He examined the roadway and thought that the dirt before his house showed unusually deep scarrings, but the tracks of hoof and wheel were like any other tracks, so he went in again, wondering that the potent and imaginative monarch of the nether regions had not bethought him to give his horse a cloven foot too—like the Hapsburgs, who distinguished their stables with horses of a special breed and color.

In the late afternoon Lucy arrived. He went down the path in some trepidation to meet her. Though he had never doubted her ability to save herself from the conflagration, he had been guilty of shockingly bad manners in not waiting to escort her home. He folded his hands and waited for her wrath to fall.

"Good grief, you look pious today," was all she said. She was heavily languid, her eyes were red and had little puffs under them. By mutual consent they sat down on the steps too tired to go any farther, and talked about the evening before. She still said nothing about the fire, she showed no interest in either his damnation or his salvation, which he thought heartless of her. At last he blurted out, "Look here, I burnt the place up, you know. What's going to happen now?"

Lucy smiled acidly. "Oh—pluming yourself on that, are you? You make me laugh. Still the boy-firebug—playing with matches! You burnt up your idea of Hell, that's all. You don't suppose you could deprive other people of theirs, do you? Did you really think you could take Hell away from both God and Satan?"

"No," said Timothy in a small voice, the Messianic note squeezed out of it. But her scathing tone vexed him, for he felt edgy himself today and thought she might have shown him some womanly consideration. He changed the subject. "By the way, I kept an eye out for Mr. Dombie, but I didn't see him anywhere. Would he have been with Sister, maybe, in the section where she lives?"

"Oh, him—" said Lucy vaguely; "he may not be there at all. He was half-dead when we knew him; there's no telling what sort of man he was before the War; very likely he was a good and brave soldier and went to Heaven when you finished him off. These war heroes are hard to get your hooks into."

"Sister did," said Timothy nastily, giving her the kind of sidelong glance he had learned from her.

Lucy colored furiously and the reddening of her skin suddenly brought out her resemblance to Sinkinda. "The men I choose aren't near-corpses—I've never fallen that low. That poor old crock was the best Penelope could get. I have a better choice; it's just a question of waiting to find a chink in people's armor, like my suspecting you had rigged up the fire at your house. Now don't ask me why, with so many livelier people to choose from, I spend my time with you; that's something I can't explain to myself, let alone anybody else."

She fanned the summery twilight air irritably, and he saw that there was earnest in her jest. "You didn't spend much time with me last evening, my girl; you preferred to move in very dubious company and cared nothing, apparently, about what happened to me."

Lucy leaned against the banisters, a sullen Pre-

Raphaelite, her nostrils flaring. After a while she offered an unwilling explanation. "I belong to that world and you'll have to accept it. You can't apply the stodgy standards of our day to a way of life that's as old as time."

Timothy took her hand. "But in the long run, Lucy, Evil is just too thick, you can't swallow it."

She shrugged. "But in the long run you couldn't swallow the 'Good' world either. You were really pretty silly last night, you know."

He looked into the creeping dusk of the garden and said, "It was quite a decision to have to make."

She slipped his hand in the open neck of her dress, and her smooth flesh sent its soft, startling communications through his fingertips. "You keep saying you want to be with me—that nothing else matters. Well—?"

He bowed his head on her shoulder. "I want to be with you forever . . . but not in that bedlam. I found I did know something about Evil—not much, but more than I realized. You must come with me, Lucy; a man's passion is stronger, it has to prevail. My idea of Good is still pretty negative, but I'm going to keep on hunting. If I could find just one moral—"

With a turn of her supple waist Lucy slipped from his grasp and jumped up. She tied on her scarf with characteristic decision. "You're an awful bore when you talk like this, Timothy, and I can't abide you—not tonight, anyway, with the weather muggy and my head aching." She ran down the steps and along the path like an undersized amazon out for the kill.

Timothy sat still and let her go.

222

After that their relationship grew more and more uneasy; the spontaneous delight drained out of it, with Timothy always trying to stop leaks that he could never find. The time for plant-collecting had passed; as the summer came on, the insect pests waxed fiercer, so they gave up the picnics. Though they rubbed themselves energetically with odoriferous leaves and lotions, mosquitoes spoiled their evenings even in the house. Lucy's lack of education began to tell; conversation became difficult—so many of his favorite topics met with blank incomprehension. In the hot weather her dress grew slovenly, she yawned in his face a great deal, and gave way to fits of childish temper. Natural behavior, he concluded, was selfish behavior; a few well-chosen conventions were essential to human relationships. . . .

She stayed away oftener nowadays, and when she was with him she seemed overcome by a greater lassitude than the weather warranted. Never to know what she did during these absences wracked him with frenzy, and to save his life he couldn't help betraying his torment. Seeing her stroll up the garden path, half reluctant, he would rush out to meet her.

"Where have you been, Lucy?"

Her eyebrows would work with resentment at being questioned. " 'Killing swine.' "

He never knew whether she was quoting a witches' jingle, punishing his curiosity, or telling the truth.

One evening he came home and found her there before him. She was darting about the garden, stalking lizards with noiseless feline pounces. As she caught the little scampering creatures she cracked their necks and dropped them into a pail. Timothy was outraged. "Don't kill my chameleons!" he exclaimed. "I love them and they don't do any harm—in fact, they do good in the garden. They eat the insects that eat the plants. I don't understand you, Lucy!"

"Oh, there you go again." She peered out at him from the bush under which she was crawling, her small face sharp with animal pursuit. "Why aren't you weeping for the poor bugs the lizards kill?"

"It's not the same thing," Timothy objected.

"Why not? Mosquitoes and mealy bugs are useful to them, and they are useful to me. If you are going to try to reform Nature, you'll be busy for quite a while. Lizards can be put to good uses in my trade, you know."

Timothy abandoned a protest inevitably lost on her. He went indoors and buried his nose in a book.

But he could not make up his mind to give her up. He still hoped the bitter hurts they dealt each other could be healed and their love restored to its former delight and tension. He tried hard to please her by bringing her presents, he tempted her appetite with fresh figs and such delicacies as the market afforded. One day he passed a fancy goods shop and saw in the window an ingenious ornament made of hair. It was a lover's wreath, the leaves and flowers cunningly varied by different shades and textures and set off by a handsome gold frame. It would delight Lucy, he thought at once; it looked like her somehow. He went in and recklessly paid the high price asked for the novelty.

When Lucy came he greeted her with loverlike warmth, and, taking the ornament from his bureau drawer, presented it to her. She glanced at him in surprise, he thought, and studied it without speaking. Timothy felt slightly miffed; "I thought you'd like it," he said pointedly.

"I do like it and it was sweet of you to bring it to me, darling. But"—she sniffed it carefully—"this person is dead. She won't do me any good—if that's what you had in mind."

Timothy snatched it from her hand and threw it on the table. "Can't you think of anything else! I hoped you'd admire its artistic qualities, but it seems you are callous to beauty that is delicate and inventive." He marched to the window and stood with his arms folded, his back to her.

He heard her go to the table, padding softly on the bare floor, and pick up the ornament. After a pause she said, "Where did you get it? Did they have any more? Usually living people sell their hair to make these ornaments. I don't know why I never thought of a hair-goods shop—"

In a jealous fury Timothy turned on her. "Lucy—are you riding other people now? Is that why you are away so much at night?"

She did not answer and he went over and took her arm. "What's come over you? You seemed happy with me, our love seemed to be a delight to you too. Why have you changed? Why do you leave me in this heartless way to go off after—I don't know what kind of strangers—" He dropped her arm and walked distract-edly up and down the room.

"I'm a hag; you have to remember that. Besides, re-lationships just do change, and jealousy is stupid; it's the most boring of all human traits. You can't hold quicksilver by squeezing it in your hand."

Timothy took a deep breath and said, "Well, if you *must* have your night-traveling, why don't you ride me again?"

She considered for a moment. Then she said, "I don't know whether you've noticed it or not, but you've stopped worrying about Penelope and about burning up the house. In spite of your craze for morals, you've managed to shed a lot of guilt in the last few weeks. That makes it harder to ride you—and less fun. The truth is," she admitted, "I have to have some hold on a person. It was probably a mistake, talking you out of so many poses; it would have been better to have left you as you were. Besides, what do I get for my pains? You won't come over and join my side, and you don't seem to like it on the other side either."

"Lucy, why don't you give up your side? Give up all this night-traveling and carousing and hell-raising, and let's settle down. Maybe it's another human weakness, but I'm beginning to want just to lead a normal life again. We could be so happy here," he urged. "We could build up our business and—well, we could get married—"

Lucy let out such a derisive screech that his eyes dropped; they fell on himself and his own absurdity.

226

He thought despairingly of the high company she was used to in Hell.

"I know I'm not exactly eligible," he admitted. "But I'm content to swap the Devil for a witch." He managed a smile. "Wouldn't you swap an enchanter for a faithful druggist?"

"Do you mean we should go into a church and have the Bible read over us? You really are a lunatic, Timothy!"

"I suppose we can't get married in a church, but there's the probate judge . . . though maybe we are not popular with the law either. I don't care, we can use some ceremony of Hell, if you like—" He paused, remembering some of the ceremonies he had seen in that particular jurisdiction and others he had guessed at.

Lucy went off into a fit of silent laughter, and it was not reassuring. "We don't have marriages in Hell any more than in Heaven, stupid; don't think they are any more advanced than we are in that respect. The idea that you can make love last forever is just a human lunacy. When the time comes for us to part, we'll part."

It won't be long, Timothy thought, in agony. He threw himself on her, his pride dissolving. "Lucy! Don't leave me, I can't go on without you now."

Lucy withdrew in a sort of repulsion from this appeal. "What's the matter with you, Timothy? First jealous and now begging. I've never been jealous and I've never groveled. It's hateful—you give me the creeps." She jumped up and shook off his unwelcome touch.

Timothy got up too, furious with himself and with her. "You are without loyalty or pity, aren't you?" he said calmly, aware above his raging heart how the very inclemency of his love was betraying him into folly and inviting catastrophe.

Lucy, he saw, found him absurd too. "I know what I want," she said crisply. "I'm sick of your moralizing and your shilly-shallying."

"Maybe you won't get it."

"Maybe not. But I go after it and that's my satisfaction."

"Well, I can't go after Evil," said Timothy sorrowfully. "I can't explain this to you, nor even to myself. It's just a feeling that at the end of the chase the beast will rend the hunter."

"Very well," said Lucy, "you've made up your mind not to come with me. That's something, at least. Go after your milk-and-honey Heaven then—if you can stomach that nasty diet. But what does God promise you? Retribution! Don't think He'll let you off from that!"

The sharp word, with its smell of brimstone, its sound of lightning and thunder, struck against Timothy's bosom, and in the moment of shock and silence that followed she spun around and ran downstairs. "Lucy! Come back!" He plunged after her in the blind fear of abandonment. In the hall below he dashed at the closed front door; it was locked, its solid panels threw him back with the violence of a blow. Lucy—how had she gotten out? . . . But what did it matter? One way

228

or another, she was gone. Stunned and dizzy, he fell back to the staircase and sat down at the foot, on the bottom step of misery and despair.

August enveloped the town in its moist sultriness. Weeds grew high in the streets that, like Timothy's, were unpaved. The sunlight hung thick from the white and yellow walls; umbrellas and parasols bobbed on the sidewalks, the horses put on their straw hats. Rather to Timothy's surprise the *News and Courier* came regularly after his break with Lucy; life went on about as usual but stripped of fear and of delight. People, he read, were flocking to meetings about the Home Rule issue, for the South naturally sympathized with Ireland's desire for autonomy, and passed resounding resolutions supporting the Irish position. President Cleveland's bride captivated the public fancy; her flounced dresses, her high-buttoned, scalloped-topped shoes, and her admiration for the novels of Ouida profoundly influenced feminine life. Families left in batches for the mountains or the islands.

It all seemed as remote to him as the Thirty Years' War. His narrow garden lay like a backwater from which he seldom put out except to the Library or to buy the necessities for existence. The popularity of Partridge's Hirsutus faded, and he thankfully gave up making nostrums, but his erstwhile customers began to look on him sullenly; he found cunjers hidden under the back steps, and anonymous notes threatened him bodily harm. He examined the account at the savings

bank, thinking that since it had been a joint enterprise
he should send Lucy her share of the earnings, but
their extravagant pleasures had nearly emptied it. So-
berly he tried to make some plan to mend his fortunes.
His life of late had unfitted him, however, for human
society, so nothing occurred to him.

Even the brindled cat had left his bed and board.
He leaned on the gate like a length of wet sacking and
poked idly among explanations of this phenomenon.
"Can familiars have kittens?" he asked the oysterwoman,
who came by with she-crabs in the R-less months. Her
whoops of uncorseted laughter shook up the lifeless air
of his small garden; between her gurglings he made out
that Old Scratch, too, had to replenish his supply of
critters, most likely by the good old sure-fire method.

It worked for the lizards at any rate, who produced
new generations of infantine dragons, and that pleased
him. Clouds of flies from his favorite neighbor, the
livery stable, pleased him less; neither sheets of flypaper
nor Pollo's languid activities with a long palmetto fly-
brush discouraged their unflagging attentions. Timothy
moved restlessly from one room to another in search of
what little breeze blew, and at times his longing for
Lucy would tear deep groans from his throat. At a noise
in the chimney he would start up in terror and hope,
but now it really was the chimney swifts, and he sank
back to the emptiness of his room where nothing ever
happened. Only the cat bone was left, forgotten on the
mantel.

More and more Timothy talked to himself. Actually

it was Lucy he talked to, or Sinkinda, remembering their words, their gestures, going over and over with them the weighty matters that rumbled in his head. Why should Retribution overtake me? Lots of people seem to escape it. Of course, a Judgment Day will come when all the accounts are in. . . . He heard the trumpet sounding, he saw the earth giving up its prisoners to the judging, and his bones turned to water.

In his gray mind only his sins made a scarlet thread. He counted them doubtfully. Shouldn't he think about repenting them? He thought about it, and found that somehow sins look more formidable after being committed. He regretted burning the Bible, an absorbing and educational book which had only been the tool of Unseen Forces. Yet it was hard to think of it as sacrilege. As to Sin in the narrow sense, he said delicately, sparing himself—for it was even harder to think of his romance with Lucy as fornication—we usually get paid off in this life, by desertion, sleepless nights, anger, and bitterness. I certainly did. Now about Sister . . . He imagined her rearing up, severity on her large eyelids, confronting him with the sin of fratricide.

Whew! he said. Then his jaw hardened. I repent some, but not all, he said. Anyway, I doubt if repentance really gets you off.

Many a night as he lay wakeful, islanded in the mosquito net, he resolved to try to find Lucy, to reason her into making a new start with him; and a despairing hope that she might be missing him as he longed for her would make his heart beat thickly. But when he came out from under the canopy in the morning he saw that it was useless; her skeptic wisdom had recognized that their moment had passed. Curiously, he never seemed to see her on the street—though possibly that was because he had grown absent-minded again, trudging with his head down the better to brood on his wretched state. Once he walked across town to the edge of Ashley River and looked at the opposite bank where they had sported in the shade. The grove glistened in summer emerald; Timothy was sick for his lost delight and cried out, "Why do we always have to pay for our fun?"

August plodded along growing heavier and grayer; even the sun had gone gray in an aged sky. At last it ended . . . tomorrow it would be September, he thought, going to bed early that evening for want of better entertainment. But what gifts could September bring to a man whose will was paralyzed by the sheer lack of friction and contrast? Under the coverlid of the heat his limbs lost the power to move, and he drifted easily into a state that was half trance and half expectancy.

This can't last, he said to himself, letting go his hold on consciousness; and as if the words had touched a secret spring, he was awake again in the rumpled bed, straining to discover what had roused him. Then he heard it far below, stirring through the deep arches of the earth. He stared about the half-lit room as if he expected the tenuous and abstract wave of sound to roll visibly through it. He felt a slight jerking, though whether of his limbs or of the house he couldn't tell.

Suddenly the rolling deepened and rushed at him; the house shook in the clutch of a giant claw. The china rattled like loose teeth, and with terrified eyes he saw the wardrobe come out from the wall in a solemn and horrible dance; he sprang up as it tottered and crashed across the place where he had lain, carrying the bed to the floor with a splintering of slats.

This escape appeared to be only momentary, for the house shook more furiously and the tiles skipped and clattered off the roof. The jarring went on in a screaming crescendo, the walls swayed inward. Flying down the steps, Timothy blessed the long practice that made his footing sure. In the lower hall the door swung open—he hadn't locked it of late, having neither hope nor fear of intruders—and he clearly heard the stamp of hoofs outside his gate. Then a whiff of burning leather came to him and he was back in the old house for a moment watching the Bible curl in the flames. He felt life pass over his head and waited for the blow to fall.

Yet the powerful instinct to run out from the plaster showering on him propelled him down the path. There was no black gig-horse in sight. The Negroes were pouring into the street in utter demoralization; across the way he saw the oysterwoman going round and round in her long white nightgown and seeming to his dazed eyes to rear up monstrous in size. She caught sight of Timothy and stopped her spinning. "De Day of Jedgment, Doctor! Oh, Jedus—come down!" Falling on her knees, she began to repent loudly a blood-curdling list of sins.

The scream of a horse shattered his nerves and he whirled about to see the livery stable afire and the hostlers dragging out the frantic animals. Mechanically he started for the stable door to help, but the horses broke away and ran wildly down the street, and he took out after them, heading for the center of town. Lucy—Lucy! he kept saying, but the pressure on his head would not let him think out her place in this catastrophe.

A dry whitish mist filled the air through which the lampposts loomed like emaciated monsters with enormously bloated heads. The earth cracked under him as he ran; the engraving in the dining room at home was coming true before his eyes. The half-naked people bursting out of doorways, the women clutching their children, the crippled carried out by their friends, a dead girl doubled against a churchyard wall . . . he knew it all from childhood. Others beside the oyster-woman screamed out embarrassing confessions and prayed for forgiveness.

Chunks of masonry clogged the roadway and slowed Timothy's pace. The white choking dust thinned suddenly and between the shreds he caught a glimpse of witchlike figures flying over a low wall. He put on speed, but couldn't come up with them. A black shrieking face with horns appeared at a cellar grating, rattled it insanely, and dropped from sight again.

He saw no signs yet of the Highnesses. Heaven had withdrawn behind the film of plaster dust; and the Monarch from below merely knocked, so far, against the crust

234

of the earth. How would death come? And at what moment? The Highnesses lacerated your nerves by not letting you know. It was not quite straightforward of them,
he thought. From present indications they would shake
down the world and its inhabitants and grind them to
rubble by slow stages.

Timothy had covered several bocks when Satan made
his presence felt again; the street rose in waves that ran
visibly before him, carrying the weightless cobblestones
on their backs. He was thrown to the sidewalk; under
his ear he heard the long muffled pounding like infernal
artillery.

The earth steadied once more. Timothy got up; his
demoralization was settling now into a sort of fatalism.
He would keep going until his call came; for his desire
to know if Lucy was safe still spurred him. Running
along the Farrs' street he quickly saw that their house,
although of clapboard, was standing; Satan had looked
out for his own. The doors hung open and he went
through the lower rooms, striking matches and calling.
But those usually crowded apartments were silent caves
that gave back nothing but a quaver of his own voice.

No neighbors could be found, either, to set him on
Lucy's tracks—indeed, the people he tried to question
in the streets were all strangers in that quarter, he gathered, having run there on the same crazy impulse that
sent everyone looking for safety somewhere else. The
probability that Lucy was well able to take care of herself brought him thin comfort—it only defined and gave
depth to the differences in their realities. He came down

the front steps of the Farrs' disordered house thinking
that his reality was to know to his marrow the sensation
of being tribeless and unfriended.

He pulled himself together and hurried toward a
large square from which a comfortingly human clamor
rose. The street lamps had gone out, but the square was
well if fitfully lighted by a row of houses ablaze along
one side. Hundreds of people had gathered there, bringing their dead and injured on mattresses, and had made
low shelters with coats and blankets. Timothy picked
his way among them, feeling that he had gone far back
in time and come on a village of barrows and cromlechs.

The Negroes had drawn to one side of the square
and, kneeling in a great congregation, begun to sing:
"We will all pray togedder on dat day . . . I'll fall upon
my knees and face de risin' sun . . . oh, Lawd, hab mussy
on me . . ." and their voices drew a long sound of beauty
and continuity through the horror. "You cyan' hide—
you cyan' hide—you cyan' hide w'en de worl's on
fiah. . . ."

Obviously you can't; yet somehow there was comfort
in the singing of it. Timothy could see no sign of Lucy,
but, wheeling this way and that, he suddenly found
himself face to face with Will Golightly. They rushed
at each other and embraced. "Thank God, you're all
right, Timothy!" Will cried. "I've been fretting about
you!" To touch Will's muscular naked shoulder, to be
fretted about, lifted Timothy on a wave of pure happiness.

The wave washed over and engulfed even Will's

family; they all shook hands with solemn cordiality. Anna Maria, always resourceful, had made them a tent from a blanket and a clotheshorse. "Where were you, Timothy," she cried, "when the first shock came? We had just finished a late supper of cold duck and were going to bed; how we got out, the good God alone knows. Our house is gone, you know, the chimney fell and split it right in two. But that's nothing, since we all escaped with our lives." She had prudently taken time to save the remains of the duck, and, looking larger than life in her cambric wrapper, she was now passing it out to her family, in which she hospitably included Timothy.

The girls, Timothy saw, had saved their new shoes; indeed, people all about them had idiotically rescued treasured articles—a sewing machine, a picture frame, a tureen from which no soup would ever be ladled. They jostled one another and exchanged rumors of buildings destroyed, friends killed, tidal waves about to engulf the town. "Hell and death," said Will, hitching up his trousers; "if your time has come to meet your Maker, it don't make a damn bit of difference if it comes with fire or with flood," and he fell to work on an unconscious woman whose limp body had been deposited near them by her husband.

Timothy squatted beside Will and held his doctor's satchel, thankful just to be near his cousin. "You know, Will, I've made up my mind about certain things: I'm convinced more than ever Evil isn't just the new idea, the challenge to the accepted Good. Of course, people hate giving up their old morals—even if they don't use them—for new ones; but Lucy was wrong. Evil is more than that."

"Lucy who?" Will gave him an abstracted glance, feeling his patient's pulse. "Here, Tim—chafe her wrists with spirits while I listen to her heart again."

Timothy, suddenly conscious of his draggled nightshirt, tucked it closer about him and attended to the lady's wrists. The smell of this liniment was so invigorating that he surreptitiously took a small swallow. His frittered mind was beginning to work again and all his natural obstinacy came out and hardened his long jaw.

"It's a dead end, that explanation of things. You begin to tolerate Evil and where do you wind up? I'm against toleration." He rubbed with evangelical zeal. "Of course the Manichaeans have a good theory. They think that Good and Evil have equal power in the world, but that someday in a great catastrophe Good will rise up and vanquish Evil." He considered this idea thoughtfully for a moment and then added, "But I wasn't raised a Manichaean, so I don't believe that. And Hell looks a lot closer than Heaven right now."

The woman moaned and came to. "Oh . . . oh . . . where am I?" She raised her head and, seeing two half-naked men bent over her, fell back in her faint again.

Timothy took advantage of her retirement from the conversation to ask quickly, "What do you think about it, Will?"

"Damn me, how should I know? All you can do is to try and keep Good ahead of the game. You have to control fifty-one per cent of the stock—that's my idea."

"It's a great idea," said Timothy, struck back on his heels, "or would be if the game weren't over. I wish you'd mentioned it before."

"God Almighty, Timothy! You're the hell of a fellow, sitting there arguing about Good and Evil in the middle of an earthquake."

"Earthquake! So that's what you think it is! It's the end of the world, man!"

As if in his support, the deep, hoarse voice began again, like the roar of the universe. The earth came loose from its foundations, and the tower of the church opposite rocked and crashed into the square. The light from the burning houses shot up; in this pallid glare they stared at each other, suspended; then it slowly dimmed in the upsurging smoke.

The fresh shock had brought the patient to her senses; she sat up between them with a quavering cry. Will helped her to her feet and turned her over to her friends. "Well, Tim—we're liable to know all the answers any minute now, so don't worry about them." And clapping his cousin on the shoulder he went bounding across the square to attend to the newly injured.

Timothy watched him go in perplexity. Dear Will, impulsive, generous, always able to escape thinking by action. And yet, suppose—good God, suppose this certainty of doom he felt was only *his* doom advancing! A hideous heresy edged into his mind: Judgment Day was an absurdity. If the dead of ten thousand years were already learning the harp or burning below, they had been judged as they fell. There would be no prisoners at the bar should a Great Day come.

This revelation knocked his underpinnings out as none of the seismic shocks of the evening had been able to do. He sat down suddenly on the grass. For in that case he was going to his appointed goal alone. Judgment Day, he saw, would have been easy by comparison; everybody would be catching it at the same time. He dropped his head in his hands and groaned for Judgment Day lost. The Highnesses, he couldn't help feeling, had done themselves out of a great show.

When the hysteria in the square had died down a little, the young Golightlys returned to the duck carcass.

"Will you be all right here?" Timothy asked, getting up. "There's something I have to do. . . ." Obviously they would do as well here as anywhere, and he took his leave. An uncontrollable restlessness had taken hold of him.

The conviction that his time had come made him feel meager and naked. One simple reason suggested itself: he looked about him and appropriated without a qualm a pair of trousers lying on the sidewalk. As he tucked his nightshirt in, the sweet solace of respectability stole over him and he went on with more confidence. The glare from the houses retreated behind him. In the quiet canal of the street he followed, he began to collect the thoughts that were bubbling up and spilling out of his head. He wanted to prepare his case, to say what he could for himself when he got down there. . . .

Between the darkness and his preoccupation he collided with a smooth hairy body—a horse being led along by a colored man. As they disentangled themselves, Timothy said, "You have to re-examine Good and Evil constantly; they change their appearances, like Satan at the reception."

The whites of the man's startled eyes showed in the dimness. "Hallelujah!" he exclaimed, and hurried away with his horse.

Timothy went on talking: "About Sister and Mr. Dombie . . . I was caught in that trap. . . . Being kind and dutiful to sisters doesn't always work out. I had to get from under. Though I chose the wrong method—you can't just kill very trying people, I suppose. You have to deal with them some other way."

Like a fresh quake under foot it came over Timothy where he was headed. Down the street a little way gaped the site of Partridge's Pharmacy. The smoke and dust seemed to take him by the throat, but some door still swung there, drawn on air, through which he had to pass, and he went on. As he came nearer he could see the brick foundations, full of charred rubble; but the horror of its ruin had diminished now, for ruin had come to join it; it had merely anticipated this night by a few months.

A column had fallen across the street from a building opposite; a fireman was putting a lantern on it to warn passers in the roadway. When the firemen had gone, Timothy took the lantern and walked along the foundation wall of the house to the gap where his bedroom had been.

The cellar was like a well; the chimney had fallen into it, but the brick arch that had been its basement support still stood and made a shallow cave against the wall. As he turned the lantern on it he saw in the arch the sharp gleam of a pair of half-moon eyes. The old stab of love and fear went through him. Then he jumped into the cellar and stumbled over the intervening bricks.

"Have you come for me, Sinkinda?"

She sat sidewise, framed in the arch like a demonic saint in a catacomb. He saw that she had on her dark green habit and her look of lazy anticipation.

"I knew you'd turn up here, sooner or later."

Timothy looked at her hopelessly. She said, "Aren't you ready to go yet? It's not very agreeable here just now."

"No, it's dreadful . . . there's nothing to stay for, God knows. And the suspense is ghastly. I want to get it over with. The only thing is, I do wish—"

Her eyebrows went up in inquiry.

"Well, it hurts a man's pride to live all his life on earth and not know whether he was right or wrong. If I only had a little more time to get my mind straightened out on that score."

"The ruling passion strong in death!" She touched him with a quick gesture that was waspish but not uncomforting. "Most people in their last moments want

242

time to be with their lovers, or just to enjoy life—but you want more time to find a moral. I will say, Timothy, that of all my victims you're the most charmingly un- expected and the most provokingly consistent."

"Thanks."

Sinkinda uncoiled herself from the arch and went off, hunting among the debris in the cellar. A little breeze brought the chink of glass and metal to him as she turned the shards of his old life. Then she came back, her bare feet making a dry whisper on the bricks, her tawny colors picking up and extending the circle of the lantern's light. She held in her hand the broken phar- macist's slate on which he used to jot down his orders. She handed it to him with the slate pencil. "Here, write your list of topics. And make haste—because the time is running out."

Timothy came to with a start and took them from her. He moved the lantern nearer, sat down, crossed his legs, and tried to concentrate. The earth had stopped shaking for a while, but he found writing difficult. "I see you have to go on without knowing. The problem is too big for our narrow experience. But in spite of all the confusion a few things remain. Senseless cruelty is bad."

He wrote it down in his crabbed script. "It bursts out now and then in the world, but, even when they prac- tice it, people recognize that it is evil. Goodness is bad- ness, sometimes . . . like Sister's pity. You were right, it was self-pity, a morbid fellow-feeling for the weak.

243

My acquiescence was bad, and the defeatism I lived in.
Murder," he admitted regretfully, "is bad. It is too easy
a way out of a situation." He wrote down murder.

"But there are some sins you can't assess. After all,
I set Hell on fire and got away in the Devil's gig. Will
that be counted against me when I get there?" Sinkinda
watched him, smiling, and offered no help. "To tell the
truth, I think I did right. That house was dreadfully
bad taste; ostentatious—and all those tricksy effects.
But there'll be another hell waiting for me. . . ."
He gave a long sigh. "There's no time now to unravel
that knot. You know, I have an idea that even Retribution can't last forever. Everlasting Hell wouldn't work:
it would cease to burn. Besides, you hellions—I don't
use the term in any disparaging sense, my dear—would
be the first to get bored with it. Being shut up there
forever with all us sinners—"

"Sinners are at least more diverting than saints," said
Sinkinda. "And now, if you've finished writing your
tablets of the law, which I must say are not original,
we'll go along, shall we?"

"It's no time to be original—when you're facing pay-
day. You just have to save what you can without vanity
of authorship. It's not much," he admitted, "in fact, it's
precious little to salvage, when life is done. But it's a
good tablet as far as it goes. I intend to hold on to it
as long as I can." He took a firm grasp on the slate and
stood up.

Sinkinda slipped an arm around his neck with the
lovingly venomous gesture that was her sign and signa-

ture. "Oh, Sinkinda! I don't know whether you are more a fiend or more a woman," said Timothy, embracing her. "If only we could have met under other circumstances! It should have been different, somehow."

"Ah, my friend, how many star-crossed lovers have uttered that cry!" She pushed him off gently.

The lantern guttered and went out of its own accord. Timothy felt the frightening and familiar weight bearing on his shoulders. As always it drove him along, it took possession of his will, his effort to shed it gave him the impulsion and the speed. He went nimbly over the bricks, sprang to the foundation wall, and ran into the street. Neither the fallen column nor the gaps in the pavement tripped his bare feet as they sped on this strange promenade. He skirted the bright patches where houses smoldered, covering the ground rapidly; far off he could see the sallow canopy hanging over the square where he had left the Golightlys. Oh, Will, he thought, shall we meet again? Maybe not. Good-by, Will. Maum Rachel I may see . . . she is in this somehow. But Pollo— it's too soon to say. Though if he keeps on telling lies . . . And Sister—will we be able to patch it up down there? Do the wrongs people do each other cancel—not only the big wrongs but the little wrongs of daily living? I sincerely repent having roasted Mr. Dombie, that poor man. I'd prefer not to meet him again—I wouldn't know how to explain things to him.

He ran on; he thought they were making a great circle through the town, but he couldn't be sure. He had lost his hold on trees and stones, all except the slate, which he went on clutching. Its jagged edges cut his fingers with a sharpness that reassured him somehow. Like an amulet of saint's toes, it clothed a belief with a shape you could hang on to through thick or thin. Retribution was going to be pretty thick, he supposed. He called Sinkinda's name once or twice, but got no answer except the low pleasureful whistling of her breath. He could feel it on his neck, yet she had become remote and inhuman, so he had to talk to himself.

I'll have to pay for my sins, of course, he said puffing a little, because his pace was fast. But Retribution argues justice somewhere in the universe. . . . He cantered along in silence for a while, thinking this over. It isn't justice, is it, to be damned for eternity when sin is so short. That's overcharging—I never did it in the shop. This struck him as a good point; he would have liked to add it to the slate, but there was no time now —fast as he ran, the last hour was running faster.

He began to notice figures ahead, apparitions that swayed in and out among the ruins with the incredible ease and suppleness of their kind. Whether any of his recent acquaintances flitted among them, he couldn't say; but the vaguely defined horns, the black pointed hats, the goatish antics of the imps, did not frighten him—indeed, their familiarity brought him a little rush of self-confidence. He couldn't help thinking that having friends in the nether regions might temper the grimness of his sojourn; his knowledge of Hell should put him in a better bargaining position when it came to demanding another chance. which he all at once resolved to do.

No doubt he'd have to be damned uncomfortable for a while, but maybe it wouldn't be so bad. And how restful to have this matter of Good and Evil settled. Suddenly he said, At any rate, I won't fear the worst, and decided to stop talking. Let those be his last words. They were capital last words, and he didn't want to spoil them.

It was only a few minutes after that, as far as he could tell, that he came to his own gate. The house was gone; where it had stood the earth had opened in a great gap; the mouth of Hell had swallowed with stark thoroughness all the furnishings, the dreams and small plush pretensions, of his life there. He stopped short with a jar on its jagged edge.

He felt Sinkinda's weight leave him, like a leaf brushed from his shoulders. In the depths of the fissure shone a blue light in which he saw hags and witches flying about. "Ride out!" cried Sinkinda, and plunged after them, leaving a long streak of kindled air behind her.

It was no harder than jumping off the roof.